The Butcher Bird

The Butcher Bird

by

Wayne Minnick

CREATIVE ARTS BOOK COMPANY
Berkeley, California • 1998

The Butcher Bird is published by Donald S. Ellis
and distributed by Creative Arts Book Company

For information contact:
Creative Arts Book Company
833 Bancroft Way
Berkeley, California 94710

For ordering information call:
1-800-848-7789
Fax: 1-510-848-4844

Graphics and Book Design by Pope Graphic Arts Center

ISBN 0-88739-157-5
Library of Congress Catalog Number 97-68997

Printed in the United States of America

for Lenore

The Butcher Bird

Chapter One

Marygold McAllister was addicted. Not to any of the common substances like tobacco, marijuana, alcohol, or cocaine, but to an activity that, in earlier times, was known as angling, but now, in Marygold's vocabulary, went by the simple term "fishing." However, unlike most dedicated anglers, she would have nothing to do with fly-fishing and bait-casting. She considered these to be lesser forms of the sport, unsuited to snaring the kind of fish she sought. She fished for nothing but blue cats—large, hulking monsters who fed on the bottom of the river and grew to weigh as much as eighty pounds. She had, in the last year, caught a sixty-pound, seven-ounce specimen and several slightly smaller ones. These past catches had spoiled her. If a fish weighed less than ten pounds, she threw it back.

Her success in catching trophy-sized fish she attributed to a secret ingredient she added to her doughballs, an enticing scent of her own devising. She was committed to the use of doughballs because all of her big ones had been caught on biscuit-sized lumps of dough skillfully tied to her hook with a web of white thread. She had tried chicken innards a few times, but garfish went wild over them, and she found no activity more frustrating than hauling in a long-nosed, bone-filled, useless trash fish, even if the taking was filled with a moment or two of excitement.

Marygold loved October. It was, in her mind, the best month of the year, a month when crisp nights and ice-blue daytime skies wrought a change that clothed the trees in hues of red, brown, yellow, and gold. The banks of the Chattahoochee became a vision to delight her eyes. Best of all, it was a month when fish awoke from their summer doldrums.

On Saturday, October fifteenth, she drove her pickup truck out Bankhead Boulevard toward the river. She turned off, just before reaching the bridge, onto a rutted lane that she followed in the direction of Fulton County Airport. She came to a sequestered spot, hidden among the trees and made impossible to penetrate, except along a hidden path known only to her, near a rampart of bramble bushes. Behind this barricade of prickly vegetation lay a large, flat rock at whose base the murky water of the Chattahoochee flowed, concealing in its depths—but visible in Marygold's imagination—a multitude of stealthy mudcats.

An old reel taped to a twelve-foot cane pole was rig enough for her needs, and, as she baited her hook, she recalled with gratification the many times it had brought her victory over a rebellious fish. In her mind, life offered no sweeter pleasure.

The dense foliage surrounding her kept Marygold from swinging her pole to cast the bait away from the bank and into deep water. She stripped about seventy feet of line from her reel, coiled it neatly on the rock, swung the bait and sinker swiftly around in a circle, and, at the right moment, released them. Far out in the Chattahoochee, she heard a muted plop as bait and sinker plunged below the surface. She was to repeat this maneuver several times, but without result.

An hour passed. In spite of the cool breeze and the appearance of an occasional anhinga—one startled as it surfaced almost at her feet—she became bored. Experience told her the signs were bad. It was going to be a good-for-nothing day. Be smart, she told herself. Go home. You haven't had a bite of any kind, not even a teaser.

She started to reel in her line. Unexpectedly, she felt something take her hook. Smiling at this last-minute stroke of good fortune, she set the hook and prepared for stubborn resistance. The thing at the end of her line, however, behaved as no catfish had ever done. No wild surging from side to side, no determined dashes for deeper water or an obstruction to hide behind, just firm resistance. Puzzled, she wound the reel, raising and lowering the tip of the pole as she recovered line until what she had hooked came slowly to the surface of the cloudy water.

"Well, I'll be damned!" she said, as her astonished eyes made out what she had caught.

Sergeant Bullard stuck his head in Detective Davis's office. "Wade, there's a lady wants to see you. Won't see anyone else. Says she's got something she's sure will interest you."

Davis sighed. Visitors carrying undisclosed burdens were a nuisance. Most were conspiracy buffs bearing "new" evidence to support their half-baked theories. Martin Luther King's murder, even though it had happened in Memphis, inspired scores of Atlanta's screwballs to peddle, earnestly, new evidence that King was murdered by a gunman other than James Earl Ray. This lady, he surmised, had found something that convinced her the courts had erred in convicting Ray or, more likely, her evidence bore on Atlanta's most recent controversial case, that of serial killer Wayne Williams, whose conviction was still being argued in bars and boardrooms.

He spoke with resignation. "Show her in," he told Bullard.

The woman who shortly appeared, bearing a longish parcel wrapped in a brown plastic garbage bag, was, Davis decided, no naive conspiracy buff. Her face was imprinted with an aspect of candor and common sense, and he thought she looked trustworthy, but remembering the unreliability of such impressions, he decided to suspend judgment until he had spoken a few words with her.

He looked at her expectantly. She, in turn, gave him a glance of frank appraisal. "Name's Marygold McAllister," she said. "I read about the way you solved the CNN bombing. Very clever work. I'm bringing this to you because it'll take a very bright man to figure out what to do about it."

Davis recalled the alleged CNN bombing with a sense of nostalgia and amusement. It was called the CNN bombing by the press, although it had absolutely nothing to do with CNN, because an employee of the City Traffic Division was parked in a CNN parking lot when a bomb planted in his car went off, killing him instantly. The murder was put down as drug related when two kilos of crack cocaine were found in the relatively undamaged trunk of the car.

Davis had broken the case the day after the bombing, much to the surprise of Homicide Division personnel and of the cynical reporters who had predicted an arrest would never be made. With satisfying contempt for the press, Davis had led a raid on an east-side apartment, arrested the two occupants, and seized plastic explosives, detonators, and wire of the kind used in the bomb.

When he was commended, he displayed admirable modesty, declaring that the case was solved more by good luck than by shrewd detective work. The anonymous phone call that had given him the names of the perpetrators and where they were to be found he kept to himself. Notwithstanding his modest posture, he managed to convey the impression that he had succeeded by exercising unspecified occult powers of reasoning.

"Thank you," Davis said. "I'm surprised you remembered—and flattered."

"I'm not flattering you," she said with a trace of impatience. "It's my habit to speak my mind."

Davis was amused but conciliatory. "I didn't mean to imply any lack of sincerity."

"No offense taken. About an hour ago," she went on, with the air of a magician about to pull off a mystifying stunt, "I was fishin' in the Chattahoochee, near the Bankhead Bridge. You'll never guess what I caught."

Something ominous, Davis thought, or you wouldn't be here. He said nothing.

McAllister paused, as if expecting Davis to venture a guess. When he remained mute, she said grumpily, "Well, I'll show you then."

She put the package on a chair, untied the string, and, with a flourish, held her catch up before Davis's eyes.

Davis could hardly have been more surprised. Though used to confronting gruesome things, he gave a start when he saw what McAllister had caught.

"What the devil?" he said. "I don't believe it."

"Can't blame you," she said. "When I first saw it, I thought it was from a department store dummy. But it's not. It's a real human arm. Touch it. It's flesh and blood."

Davis recoiled at the prospect of touching the odious thing, but he forced himself to poke at it gingerly. He guessed it was from a human female. It had a small wrist and slender fingers; its nails were covered with red polish. He guessed it was the arm of an adolescent or a young woman. Wrapped around it was what looked like strips of lead.

"What's that stuff wrapped around it?" he asked, not expecting an answer.

"It's came," she said. "It's sold in crafts stores to people who make stained glass windows."

"How do they use it?" Davis asked, still unenlightened.

"It's a lead channel that's used to hold the pieces of a stained glass window together. The strip is joined in the center but has a groove on either side. Here, look at the end. It's like the letter *H* turned sideways."

Davis looked, then he felt the stuff. The strip was soft and pliable.

One could easily wind it around a cylindrical object like an arm.

"It's handy to weigh down something you want to sink in the river," he said. "But it's an odd thing to choose."

"It is," McAllister said. "Most people would have tied something heavy to the arm, like a concrete block." She paused, thinking. "If he had, I never would have caught it. I couldn't have hauled up a concrete block with the fishin' rig I've got. I suppose we ought to thank the murderer for using it."

"Why do you think there's been a murder?" Davis asked.

McAllister snorted in disbelief. "What else? Somebody's arm is cut off and tossed into the river. You think the victim was alive when she lost the arm?"

"Probably not. But she might not have been murdered. Maybe she died of some disease or was killed in an accident."

"Could have been," she admitted. "But why cut off the arm? Doesn't make sense." Her face expressed her perplexity. "Why mutilate a dead body? I can't see any reason for it."

"Neither can I," Davis said. "By the way, Mrs. McAllister—"

"*Ms.* McAllister," she interrupted. "I'm not married."

"Okay, Ms. McAllister." He watched her face carefully as he posed his question. "In the situation you found yourself, recovering a human arm and harboring a suspicion of murder, as you did, why didn't you call the police to the crime scene and wait there until they arrived?"

McAllister responded, resentment in her voice, "Huh! What crime scene? There wasn't any crime scene for you fellows to inspect. Unless you could somehow get to the bottom of the Chattahoochee, about eighteen or twenty feet deep."

Davis smiled. He admired her spunk. She had, he admitted, behaved as reasonably as anyone could have expected.

"No problem," he told her. "We appreciate your cooperation. If you'll come with me, I'll have a secretary take your statement. After you sign it, you can go. If you like, I'll let you know how we dispose of the case."

"I'd like that. I don't see what you can do with nothing but a dismembered arm."

"Frankly," Davis said, "it will be a challenge."

He spent little time wrestling with the problem, however. When McAllister had given her statement and signed it, he decided to confer with the division head, Gerald Fillmore. Fillmore, now about fifty years old, had risen, in accord with the way things happen in complex organizations, to a level that challenged his competence. He had been a good street cop. His performance on the beat was so extraordinary, his superiors singled him out for rapid promotion. In spite of his mediocre performance as head of the Homicide Division, the level at which he finally ended up, he still enjoyed the respect, if not the adulation, of rank and file officers. The event that had earned him such enduring regard was a dramatic one.

Every new recruit in the division had heard the story. It had gained a few dubious details from frequent telling, but knowledgeable sources still agreed that it retained the basic truth. As the story went, Fillmore and another cop, who was nicknamed Billy Blunderbuss because of his chronically poor marksmanship, answered a domestic violence call in a run-down section of southeast Atlanta. When they entered the house, they found a woman sitting on the floor of the living room, holding a crying baby, and cursing someone named Swede for having beaten her up. Blood was seeping from her nose and mouth, and one eye was almost swollen shut.

"Who done this?" asked Billy Blunderbuss, affecting a syntax he thought suitable to the situation.

"Swede. He hit me."

"And where's Swede now?"

"In the bathroom."

Fillmore rapped on the bathroom door. "Swede, this is Officer Fillmore. I'd like a word with you."

Because they had been instructed to avoid threatening behavior on domestic violence calls, neither officer had drawn his weapon. They waited for Swede to come out, expecting sullen but peaceful compliance. Swede, in a surprise maneuver, flung the door open violently, seized Fillmore in a bear hug, and, before either officer could react, pressed a straight-edged razor to Fillmore's throat.

"Don't neither of you touch them weapons," he said, "or I cut this guy's throat."

Billy froze. Fillmore struggled briefly but gave up when Swede yanked his head back sharply, causing his Adam's apple to stick out prominently. To show his determination, Swede pressed the razor so tightly to Fillmore's throat that a tiny drop of blood appeared. Billy stared at that crimson drop helplessly, unable to think of any effective way to help his partner.

Swede spoke to Billy, "You! Don't do nothin' dumb. Jist put your hands behind your head, walk out that door, git in your car, and drive away. I have to think what I'm gonna do with your buddy. Maybe I'll cut his throat. Maybe I won't. I ain't sure."

Despite his belligerent tone, he seemed nervous, unsure. The menacing stare he fixed on Billy seemed mostly bluff. He acted like a man who had got himself in a fix and couldn't figure how to get out of it.

Billy was about to obey Swede's order to clear out when Fillmore said, "Stay where you are, Billy. Swede, you listen to me. Cops don't take this kind of shit from nobody. You may cut my throat, all right, but it will cost you your life, because Billy will shoot you dead."

"I got you in front of me. How's he gonna shoot me? He gonna shoot through you?" Swede laughed.

"Exactly," Fillmore said. "You're gonna cut my throat anyway, so what have I got to lose? I'm gonna give Billy three commands: ready, aim, and fire. When I say fire, if you haven't let me go, he'll shoot right through me. The bullet that gets me is gonna get you, too. Understood?"

"Bullshit," Swede said. "Ain't nobody that crazy."

"Okay," Fillmore said. "Let's find out."

He gave Billy an odd look and a slight wink. "Ready!" he commanded.

Billy drew his gun. Swede held tightly to Fillmore, but his face was furrowed with worry lines.

Fillmore gave the second command, "Aim!"

Billy raised his weapon with both hands and pointed it squarely at the middle of Fillmore's chest.

Speaking calmly, as if he were dealing with a matter of no consequence, Fillmore said, "In ten seconds, Swede, I'm gonna give the command to shoot, and when I do, you're a dead man."

Sweat erupted on Swede's brow. There was a tremor in his voice as he said, "Now jist a minute—"

Abruptly, Fillmore shouted, "Fire!" and slumped like a sack of cement. As he fell from the startled Swede's arms, the razor slashed a bloody but superficial gash in his cheek.

Billy fired. The bullet hit Swede in the shoulder, twisting him around and tumbling him backward though the bathroom door into the tub. He lay there groaning, whimpering for help.

Swede's woman, still crouched in the middle of the floor clutching the baby, raised her head, cursed Billy, and spat on his shoes.

"She sure knew how to swear," Billy said later

When the incident was reported, everyone wanted to know if Billy really would have shot through Fillmore's chest to kill Swede, but all Billy would tell them was, "I knew it wouldn't come to that." Then he'd grin and say, "Besides, if it had, I probably would have missed."

Davis faced Fillmore, to whom he had come for advice on disposing of, literally and procedurally, the dismembered arm, and remembered the story and marveled at the man's hubris. Never in a million years would he have taken such a risk. Histrionics, he assured himself, belong in the theater, not on a cop's beat. Nevertheless, he admitted Fillmore's bravado had made him a kind of police officer's icon, an image he clearly relished. He bore the scar on his cheek like a medal of valor. Davis swore he sometimes used makeup to accentuate it.

Fillmore now doodled methodically on a note pad as he grappled with the problem of the severed arm. "We could send it to the morgue and forget about it," he mused. "Tell them to try matching it with any available stiffs they've got in the cooler. That would get it off our hands."

Davis, unconvinced of the wisdom of such action, adopted a skeptical look. "Yeah, we could do that . . ." He let his voice trail off in a carefully contrived tone of uncertainty.

"Of course, it's a fair implication that a murder has taken place," Fillmore said, scowling at Davis's covert display of disapproval, "and that places it squarely in our jurisdiction. So you'd better see if you can locate the body this member came from."

Davis was not sure how to go about locating the body that matched the arm, but Homicide Division had to cope with murder—assuming a murder had been committed—in whatever form it appeared. He was ready to give this odd case a try.

"Any ideas where I ought to look first?"

"Why not the river?" Fillmore said. "That's where the arm came from. Maybe the rest of her is down there, too."

"Thanks a lot, Gerry," Davis said, grinning derisively. "I just can't see dragging five or six miles of the Chattahoochee on the off chance we might find a body."

"Well, you asked, didn't you? Tell you what. I'll give you a helper. We've just been assigned a new recruit. Moved up from the street. Black woman. A looker with brains. Got a bachelor's degree from the

U. of Georgia and an M.S. in criminology from Florida State. Like I said, brains but no experience in homicide. How would you like to teach her the ropes?"

"It's a pleasure I could forgo. She'll probably be a pain in the ass."

"Don't be so enthusiastic. You might learn to like her."

Davis stood up. He was a big man, almost six-feet, three-inches tall, with a lean, wiry frame to match. Although his full name was Bryan Wade Davis, he despised the name Bryan, and, in deference to his wishes, his colleagues called him Wade. Many, however, thought him a bit too refined for a policeman. He liked classical music, bought tickets to the concerts of the Atlanta Symphony Orchestra, and patronized legitimate theater. He had once remarked to a fellow officer, Albert Saffron, how privileged he felt to have seen *Driving Miss Daisy* and *Steel Magnolias* long before they were made into movies. Saffron had understood the feeling, but other colleagues did not.

As Davis turned to leave, Fillmore said, "This is her first day in the division. Try being nice."

"Am I ever anything else?"

Davis sought out Leda Fulford, new recruit. He found her to be beautiful, as Fillmore had promised, but not in the fashion of the Hollywood archetype. Her nose was a bit wide, her cheekbones a bit high, and her teeth a bit irregular. But these imperfections detracted nothing from the impact of her full, sensuous lips, her dark eyes, her lustrous reddish-black hair, her creamy brown skin, and her model's body. She was striking. Davis was impressed.

"Fillmore says you and I are to work together for a while. I hope that meets with your approval."

She gave him a look of swift appraisal, as if she were interviewing a job applicant. She smiled and spoke in a half serious tone, "Wouldn't you be surprised if I said, 'No, I don't want to work with you'?"

Davis laughed. "Not only surprised, but disappointed. Do you always speak your mind like that?"

She hung her head, embarrassed. "No, sir. Not really. It just sort of popped out. I'd be honored to work with you."

Davis thought she was probably quite shy, ill at ease, trying to establish rapport with him in a misguided way. He sought to reassure her. "No offense taken," he said. "Just don't surprise me too often."

She dropped her eyes, appearing crestfallen. He couldn't tell if she was really contrite or just acting.

He told her about the arm, how it was found, and what their mission was.

"I'm stumped," he said. "Why would anyone cut the arm off a murdered body and toss it into the Chattahoochee River?"

He let his imagination, normally kept under tight rein, soar freely. Unfortunately, it provided little in the way of plausible explanations.

"The only thing that makes sense to me," he told Leda, who sat silently listening to his monologue, "is that we're dealing with a lunatic. You have to be crazy to do something like that. Only a person with a deranged mind would mutilate a corpse. I've heard that sexually violent men sometimes resort to mutilation and dismemberment after raping a woman. Especially if they're on drugs."

"So have I," Fulford said, shaking her head in doubt. "It's just that I'm reluctant to believe we're dealing with some kind of sociopath. I don't want to believe the only possible explanation for this crime—I assume we're dealing with an actual crime—is that it was done by some kind of nut."

Davis got up, walked a few paces back and forth, then sat down. His office offered no greater ambulatory scope than a lion had in a roadside zoo. But it was enough to relieve his tension.

"Can't agree with you, Leda. If lopping off the arm of a corpse is not the behavior of a nut, then tell me why a reasonable person would do it?"

Fulford smiled at him. "I can think of one or two reasons. Farfetched, perhaps, but still reasons. This is the arm of a young girl. Maybe it was cut off to provide a horrible object lesson to someone. Remember the horse's head in *The Godfather*? It was put in a man's bed to let him know what was in store for him. Well, suppose some mafia type—we've got them in Atlanta, haven't we?—decided to use the girl's arm to intimidate someone. You know, throw it on the front porch with the morning paper. Message: If you don't cooperate, the next arm you find on the front porch may be your daughter's."

Davis looked at her with feigned admiration. "You know, Leda, I admire your ingenuity. You're not really serious, are you?"

"Well," she said smiling, "you asked why a sane man might have cut off the arm. I gave you one reason."

"You certainly did." He chuckled. "I'll file it away where it belongs."

He stood up, stretched, sat down, leaned back, and stared at the ceiling. "I don't have much enthusiasm for this assignment. With nothing but a severed arm to go on, I haven't the slightest idea how to proceed. Well, that's not exactly right. I suppose the first thing we ought to do is try to find the body the arm came from, assuming the murderer didn't dismember the whole body and scatter the parts. If he had," Davis said thoughtfully, "other parts would have turned up by this time."

"Maybe," Fulford said, "there is some peculiarity about the arm that would help us. Suppose the murderer wanted to prevent positive identification of the body. Let's say, just for argument's sake, the victim's face is so mutilated as to be unrecognizable, but there's something distinctive about the arm. Something like a tattoo, or a deformity of some sort, like a crooked finger. By removing the arm and disposing of it in the river, the killer hoped the victim's identity would never come to light."

Davis thought Fulford's suggestion made sense. It could easily be checked. He was ready to give it a try, though he was pessimistic about the outcome.

"The arm is now in our morgue, in the custody of Christopher McCalmon, our medical examiner. You ought to meet him. I think you'll like him."

He paused, thinking of the wisdom, or lack of it, in what he was about to say. "He's a black man."

She gave him a peculiar look. "So?"

"Well," he said lamely, "I thought you'd like to know."

Their visit to McCalmon's morgue was delayed for three whole days.

For two of those days, McCalmon was tied up in court, testifying in cases of vehicular homicide. On the third day, Davis was called out to the scene of a revenge killing that had escalated into hostage taking. He took Fulford along.

As they sped in a red-and-white toward a branch office of the State Unemployment Agency, Davis told her what he knew of the situation. "An employee, a white male, twenty-eight years old, who had been discharged a week ago, appeared in his former boss's office shortly after lunch. He had a semiautomatic pistol and proceeded to shoot his former employer in the head. In the panic that followed, he killed a secretary, grabbed a computer analyst, a woman, and retreated to a conference room. He's there now, threatening to kill the woman if the police come near him."

"What are we supposed to do?" Fulford asked. "Doesn't the department have personnel specially trained to deal with this kind of situation?"

"There's a SWAT team there now. Also hostage resolution people. I guess we're supposed to observe and clean up the bodies when it's all over."

They drew up in front of the Unemployment Agency office and sat behind a ribbon of yellow tape that had been strung as a barrier to prevent bystanders, press, and other curiosity seekers from endangering themselves by approaching the building.

They got out of their car and stood looking at the scene. For a time, all they saw was a building that looked deserted, with no people coming and going through the doors, no activity visible within.

Then the front door opened and a man appeared, holding a woman in a tight embrace, pushing her forward as he held a gun against the back of her head. He was shouting, "I'll not hurt her if you let me get out of here. That's my car there, the green Mustang. Let the two of us get in and drive away. If you don't follow me, I'll release her, unharmed."

Fulford looked at Davis, her face a study in uncertainty. "Will they do that, Wade? He sounds as if he means what he says. The police can easily pick him up after he releases the woman."

"If you were the woman," Davis replied, "would you want to get into a car with a demented killer and drive away from police presence?"

"I suppose not," said Fulford. "But I don't see what good the police presence is doing her now."

As she spoke, the gunman and his hostage drew closer. She could see the terror in the woman's face and the desperate, dreadful mien of her captor.

Abruptly, she heard a noise like a light bulb breaking, and, as that strange sound rang in her ears, she saw the head of the gunman explode. A mass of crimson liquid, hair, and tissue flew through the air. The captive fell to the ground, screaming hysterically, her face, hair, and white blouse covered with blood and tissue.

Davis, momentarily shocked, heard a retching sound come from Fulford's throat, but in the next instant, before he could move to intercept her, he saw her leap over the tape, run to the fallen woman, lift her, cradle her in her arms, stroke her cheek, and speak soothingly to her.

A voice at Davis's side inquired, "What officer is that?"

Davis turned, surprised, to look into the face of Atlanta's Chief of Police, Bernard Schlessinger.

"She's Detective Leda Fulford of Homicide Division."

"What in the hell's she doing here?"

"I got a call on the incident and answered it. She's my colleague. I brought her along."

He seemed entranced by the scene, as if something about it surpassed his expectations. He watched Fulford rock the woman in her arms and gently stroke her cheeks. He heard her comforting voice. He nodded obliquely at Davis and spoke approvingly, "Not many women would wade into blood and gore like that."

"No, sir."

"Tell Gerry Fillmore I said she should be commended." He paused, as if about to add an important afterthought. "And see the division picks up her dry cleaning bill."

"Yes, sir," Davis replied.

Medics quickly clustered around the two women, ready to take care of the frightened hostage. Davis lifted Fulford to her feet and, arm around her shoulders, guided her to the car.

Once inside, she began to cry.

From that day forward, Leda Fulford acquired a legion of admirers throughout the division. Not the least of them was Wade Davis.

Christopher McCalmon laid the arm on a marble slab that abutted a sink with a large drain at its bottom. Above the slab, hot and cold spray nozzles hung from flexible hoses. They were there to facilitate the flushing away of blood and debris that accumulated during autopsies.

McCalmon was young, perhaps twenty-five or thirty, slender waisted and broad shouldered. Round of face and coarse featured, he was handsome in a rugged sort of way. His skin, like Fulford's, was a warm ivory-brown, his hair a thatch of loosely woven curls. He carried himself with the assurance of a man who, in a position that demanded learning and intelligence, had demonstrated he had those qualities in abundance.

"This is where I perform my postops," he said to Fulford with what might have been an attempt to impress her, but it could have been nothing more than polite commentary. There was genuine respect in his eyes, however, as he said, with obvious approval, "I hear you got commended for your part in that hostage shooting."

"Yeah. And got my uniform cleaned for free. How about that?"

"Unheard of in this penny-pinching place. Congratulations. You deserved it." Then, looking at her in an inviting way, he added, tongue in cheek, "If you ever get tired of trotting around with this big, dumb detective, consider working with me for a while. I can't tell you how much fun it is exploring the viscera of a ten-day-old corpse."

"I'll bet," Fulford replied. "Sounds enchanting. Do you suppose I could start with something fresher, though, say a corpse that's only a couple of days old?"

"For you," he gave her a charming smile, "a fresh, frozen one. Perfectly preserved."

Davis hated to admit it, but he felt a twinge of jealousy when he saw how McCalmon was drawn to Fulford and the frank way he sought to engage her interest. He could not understand his feeling. He had known the woman just a few days, but when he had watched her run to the help of the woman hostage and cradle her in her arms, in spite of her gore-spattered condition, he knew what he felt for her was growing into something beyond a proper, professional interest. A strange ambivalence came over him as he watched her dally with McCalmon.

"Hey, you two, let's get back to business," he said.

"There's no business that can't wait for a little monkey business," McCalmon declared, but he soon became serious. "You asked me if there was anything about this arm, anything that might offer a clue to the owner's—if that's the right word—identity. The answer is no. There's nothing about this arm that's distinctive. Anatomically speaking, that is," he paused.

Davis looked at him quizzically, puzzled by the remark. "Anatomically speaking? What the devil does that mean?"

"It means that it's a perfect specimen of a human arm. The arm of a young woman, maybe twenty years old, maybe a little less. No abnormality, deformity, or environmentally induced peculiarity such as a scar, tattoo, or broken bone that might lead to her identity."

"So, we're up the creek," Davis said.

"Not entirely. There's something quite remarkable about this arm." He paused to give weight to what he was about to say. "It's been embalmed."

Davis looked at Fulford with raised eyebrows. Her face registered surprise, astonishment.

"What made you believe it was embalmed?" Fulford asked. "It looks, well, natural to me."

"That natural look, as you call it," said McCalmon, "was what aroused my suspicion. Here's an arm that was amputated some days ago. We don't know how long, but it had to be quite a while. It's been immersed in the river, probably for several days. It should show signs of decomposition, evidence of being nibbled at by fish or crabs. But it doesn't. It's beautifully preserved. Why? Because it's been treated with chemicals, probably formaldehyde. I did a simple test that confirmed the presence of formaldehyde and phenol in the arteries, the usual fluids used in embalming."

"I'm thinking about the implications of your disclosure," Fulford said. "Do you think we're dealing with grave robbery?"

"As I see it, there are two possibilities. Someone could have amputated the limb from a body as it lay in a mortuary, or, what seems more likely, someone, as you suggested, Leda, dug up a body and mutilated it."

Davis considered those grisly alternatives, trying to imagine why someone would undertake to do such a thing. When Marygold McAllister had first laid the arm on his desk, he thought it had been removed from a murdered body, and even then he could think of no good reason for such an act. Now his puzzlement was compounded by the fact that the arm had assuredly come from a corpse that, most likely, had been removed from a grave.

"Chris," he asked, "do you have any idea how long ago the body from which this arm came was embalmed?"

"Not an accurate idea," Chris replied. "You see, the problem is decomposition. It gives us a clue to how long a body has been dead, but it's arrested by embalming. After the passage of months or years, an embalmed body begins to dry out. But this thing has been in the water. I'm sorry, but I can't tell you much. The body could have been embalmed as early as a few days ago, or even a year ago, maybe more, depending on where it's been."

"That doesn't help us much in trying to determine when the grave robbery occurred, does it?"

"Look, Wade, if you dug up a body, you wouldn't want to keep it around indefinitely, would you?" McCalmon said. "You'd use it for whatever purpose it served, then you'd get rid of it. Maybe this perpetrator wanted to get rid of the body by dismembering it and scattering the parts. I wouldn't be surprised if you find more parts before long."

Davis shook his head. "I don't think so. We've had the arm for a week now. If the person who cut it off had dismembered the body further, other parts would have shown up by now."

"Well then, I'd get busy looking for the rest of her," McCalmon said. "If you find her, you should have a clue as to who the perpetrator is and possibly as to why he dug her up."

"Very helpful suggestion, Chris, but I see a big stumbling block," Fulford said. "How, in the name of all that's holy, do we go about finding the body?"

McCalmon threw his hands in the air in a gesture of futility. "What I'm about to suggest doesn't seem very promising, but I can't think of any other way to proceed."

Davis cut in. He didn't want McCalmon to impress Fulford with superior judgment. He felt a little ashamed of his motive but wasn't deterred by the feeling. "I'm way ahead of you, Chris. You're going to suggest we talk to the caretakers of Atlanta cemeteries to see if they've had a recent grave robbery."

"Bingo," Chris said. "Two great minds stumbling upon the same dazzling vision."

"Wait just a minute, you guys," Fulford said with a smile. "Make that three great minds. Even I'm smart enough to think of that one."

Chapter Two

Davis's telephone conversation with Fenwick Cooper, administrator of Willow Rest Cemetery, one of Atlanta's largest, was typical of the conversations he had with the other cemetery officials he had contacted. He identified himself, explained the nature of his mission, and asked, "Have you had, in recent days or weeks, a grave robbery?"

The tension in Cooper's voice suggested to Davis that he was not at all happy to field such a question. Nevertheless, when he replied, he was controlled and unemotional.

"Mr. Davis, to my knowledge there has never been a grave robbery at Willow Rest. We put up an eight-foot wrought-iron fence around the perimeter of the grounds that is almost impregnable. The bars comprising the fence curve outward at the top, presenting a menacing row of razor-sharp teeth. Scaling such a fence would require an unimaginable feat of gymnastics."

"Certainly a daunting obstacle," Davis said, "but determined human beings have been known to overcome some pretty hazardous barriers. Can you say for sure your fence has never been breached?"

"Not with absolute certainty. However, if someone got in and disturbed a grave, our grounds crew would have detected it, even if the robber took pains to conceal his work. The soil of a disturbed grave would tend to sink, and uprooted sod would not look the same as the surrounding grass. Our gardeners would surely detect such signs."

"But you have a large number of graves, don't you?"

"We have over five thousand graves, and more are added regularly. True, we don't inspect each one on a daily basis, but if you've ever attended a funeral, you know that a fresh grave looks quite different than the older ones. If someone disinterred a body and refilled the grave, the refilled grave would stand out like a sore thumb."

Davis had a nagging feeling that Cooper was not being entirely forthcoming. Perhaps the disappointing implications of Cooper's information made him feel that way. If stealing a body from a cemetery posed such a problem, where had the arm, taken from a young woman's body, come from? He refused to believe the most likely alternative—that the body had been stolen from a mortuary. That would have given the perpetrator greater difficulty than stealing it from a cemetery. Such a theft would not have been missed by the press and would have resulted in a media frenzy characterized by garish headlines such as "The Night of the Body Snatchers."

Before he gave up the idea of the body having come from a cemetery, another possibility occurred to him. "Mr. Cooper, some people are laid to rest in . . . uh . . . above-ground tombs, aren't they."

"You mean a mausoleum? Yes. Our cemetery maintains a communal mausoleum. It's a structure that has spaces families may purchase who want above-ground burial but don't want the expense of building an individual crypt. If you're thinking one of these may have been broken into without our detecting it, I would have to say it's possible, but most unlikely. Most such structures, ours included, have heavy exterior doors and secure locks. The same is true of the individual crypts. A break-in would be quickly detected by our staff or by the family of the deceased. We've never had any evidence of an attempted break-in since I've been in charge of the cemetery."

"Well, it seems I'm on the wrong track," Davis said. "Trouble is, I don't know what other track to take."

Cooper sought to be helpful. "Have you ever thought the body might have been stolen from a mortuary."

"Yes," Davis said dryly. "The thought has occurred to me. But thanks for the suggestion. And for your time."

He hung up the phone with a heavy sigh.

As he read the medical examiner's report, Davis raised his eyes and glanced covertly at Leda Fulford. There was something about her, some feline charm, that was beginning to penetrate the wall of detachment he had erected around himself after the death of his wife two years ago. During their marriage, he and Nora had fallen into a kind of voluntary exile in which they found fulfillment only in each other. Except for rare occasions, they closed the door to friends and acquaintances and kept to themselves.

After Nora's death, Davis discovered the penalty entailed by such self-imposed exile. Cloistered alone in misery, he floundered in depression, unable to find pleasure and purpose in his life. Now, to his surprise, Leda Fulford was awakening in him a new need for friendship and love.

Leda caught his glance.

"What is it, Wade?" she asked.

He was ashamed to admit he only wanted to look at her. He pretended he needed advice.

"Cyrus Orovac and I have been talking to administrators of several Atlanta cemeteries, and we get the same story from all of them. Grave robberies are almost impossible. Security measures are too tight, and any tampering with a grave is easily detectable. Our precious arm, therefore, can hardly have come from a cemetery.

"I don't know what direction to take next. I refuse to believe a body could have been stolen from an undertaker. Think of the publicity such a theft would have aroused."

"You're assuming the theft would have been discovered," Fulford replied. "But I can think of a possible, though perhaps fanciful, way by which a body might be stolen and not discovered."

"Such as?"

"If a body is not to be viewed, it's left closed up in a coffin in the mortuary 'til the day of burial. What's to prevent a thief from breaking into the funeral home, removing the body, and reclosing the coffin. The empty casket would be buried, and no one would be the wiser, would they?"

Davis admitted the suggestion was feasible but discounted its plausibility. "You know, Leda," he said, "that's a possibility, but you're forgetting the difficulties the robber would have to face. First of all, coffins are hard to open. They're closed with latches and screws that can't be removed without special tools. And then there's the problem of weight. If the mortuary crew lifted an empty coffin, they'd know, because of its lightness, that something was wrong."

"Well," Fulford said with spirit, "the guy would probably anticipate those problems, get himself the necessary tools, and have a couple of sandbags to throw in the coffin."

"I find that hard to believe," Davis said, shaking his head in doubt.

She looked at him soberly and replied, "Maybe that particular scenario won't fly, but I offered it merely to show there may be ways of robbing a mortuary we haven't thought of."

"All right. You've convinced me there may be some robbery

schemes we haven't thought of. I'm willing to submit the question to an expert, to an undertaker who knows the ins and outs of mortuary procedure. I have a feeling, though, we'll get no more out of the effort than we did with the graveyard people."

"You're probably right, but at least it will close some doors," she said. "Save us from running up blind alleys." She paused, seemingly amused at what she had just said. "How's that for mixing metaphors?"

"Won't hold a candle to my best," Davis replied. "Since it's your baby, why don't you flip through the yellow pages, pick an undertaker with the biggest ad, and get an appointment to talk with him or her, personally. A face-to-face meeting is more likely to produce results than a telephone conversation."

Fulford searched the yellow pages for an impressive funeral home ad and came across a notice for the Cawthon School of Burial Science, which advertised itself as the South's biggest provider of instruction in disposing of the dead. A graduate of CSBS, the ad declared, would know mortuary science in all its intimate details. Looking at the ad and wondering about the kind of intimate details one might discover from a visit to the institution, Fulford decided CSBS would be a better source of information than Davis's proposed visit to an undertaker.

"Look here, Wade," she said, showing him the ad. "I think we'd do better talking to these people than to a mortician. If we knew exactly what happens to a body from the time the undertaker picks it up until it's buried or cremated, we'd have a good idea of the places in the process where it might be possible to steal the corpse."

"Makes sense, Leda. Give those people a call. Ask them to let us know when we can monitor the handling of a body through the whole process of getting it ready for the grave."

He paused, his face wearing an expression of distaste. "I don't relish watching some poor stiff being readied for his last ride. It'll be hard on my stomach. I hope we'll learn something from it."

He looked at Leda and said thoughtfully, "I see no reason why both of us have to go through this unpleasant chore. You've got other work to do. Why don't you stay here and tend to it. I promise to give you a vivid report when I get back."

Although she knew he was motivated by misguided kindness, the remark irritated her. "Wade, I could almost get mad at you. You know what you sound like? The big, brawny male sacrificing himself to shelter the fragile female who's too delicate for such ugly stuff. Well, baloney. Anything you can do, I can do."

Davis was startled. "Hey," he said, "I didn't mean to suggest you weren't up to the dirty side of police work. You can probably wade through shit as well as any man. I just thought there was no need for both of us to get our feet dirty. Okay?"

She smiled. "I forgive you. Just watch it, that's all."

He decided to tease her a bit. With a sly yet playful grin, he said, "You know, you're beautiful when you're mad. A real turn-on."

She realized what he was doing. "You've picked a dangerous way to get turned on," she said, tongue in cheek. "If you get me real mad, I might cause you to blow a fuse."

Before visiting the Cawthon School of Burial Science, Davis was summoned by Gerald Fillmore. Fillmore was a hands-on administrator, and though he gave his detectives free rein in conducting an investigation, he couldn't keep his distance for long. Instead, he sniffed around, checking progress or lack of it, offering suggestions and diagnoses, and generally, in the minds of many, making a nuisance of himself.

Davis had never found him a nuisance. In fact, he often profited from his ideas and reaped the benefit of his occasional insights, judgments that helped make order out of a mishmash of facts. He remembered vividly the suggestions he had received from Fillmore in the case of Martha Brooks, convicted killer of hospice patients.

However, Fillmore did, at times, test Davis's patience with his tendency to overdramatize mundane events. He liked nothing better than to call a press conference in the midst of a noteworthy case and interpret for reporters ordinary feats of investigation as incredible leaps of logic. He would portray criminals as satanic monsters and officers of the law as avenging angels and intellectual giants. Few reporters were taken in by such bombast.

"How are you making out in the case of the missing arm?" he now asked Davis.

"It would be more accurate," Davis replied, "to speak of a missing body than a missing arm. After all, we've had the arm in our possession for over a week."

"I was speaking," Fillmore said archly, "from the standpoint of the as-yet-undiscovered body, not from the viewpoint of the arm." Fillmore's smile was condescending, indicating that, in his mind, he had scored a great grammatical victory.

"Ah," said Davis, "I see." His smile was benign, as if to say he intended no offense in making the correction. "To return to the question. We have made, I must admit, little progress. A diligent investigative effort has convinced us that the arm, which was embalmed, as you may have learned, probably did not come from a grave robbery. Tomorrow, Leda and I are going to look into the possibility that it might have been stolen from a mortuary. We expect negative results."

Fillmore listened attentively. He tore a sheet covered with intricate doodles from his memo pad and began decorating a fresh sheet. "You've looked in the obvious places, and I'm assuming you're right about your mortuary visit bearing negative results. What then?"

"Well, there's one more place, a very unlikely place, I admit, from where a body could have been stolen. I'm talking about a medical school's dissecting room, where students learn anatomy by cutting up cadavers."

Fillmore nodded sagely, as if the idea had been in his mind all along. "Good thinking. I'd guess it would be easier to steal a body from there, or part of a body like an arm, than from a graveyard or a mortuary."

Davis nodded. "On the face of it, yes. But medical schools must have strict security measures. They have to depend heavily on donated bodies. It would cause a hell of an uproar, for example, if the parents of a teen-ager, who had donated their child's body for medical research, were to find a part of the body floating down the Chattahoochee."

"Granted," Fillmore said. "You'll look into it, won't you, after you've done your thing at the mortuary?"

Davis assured him a visit to Southeastern Medical School was in the works. He took the opportunity, however, to air his doubts about the amount of time and effort being spent on the case.

"Gerry, I've had reservations about the importance of this case ever since the medical examiner told us the arm had been embalmed," he said. "When that lady, Marygold McAllister, brought it into my office, I was sure we were on to a murder. After all, a severed arm suggests the owner didn't lose it voluntarily, or while fully conscious. Therefore, she must have been killed before she was mutilated. But if the arm's been removed from an embalmed body, the presumption of murder evaporates. The worst sort of criminal behavior we can now assume is grave robbery or—and I don't know if this is an actual crime—the desecration of a corpse."

Fillmore scratched his chin and nodded. "You've got a point. Unless something happens to change things, we'll file the case under fascinating puzzles and forget it. In the meantime, you may get some help from this."

He pushed a copy of the local newspaper across the desk to Davis.

"A reporter was nosing around the division yesterday, looking for a story, and I thought I would ask him to give us some help. He was cooperative. In fact, I practically wrote the story for him."

Davis read, with some consternation, a story that detailed the discovery of the arm, revealed the assumption that a murder had been committed, and asked that people having any knowledge bearing on the case to contact Detective B. W. Davis of Homicide Division.

"You will note," said Fillmore, "that I wrote this thing while we were under the impression a murder had been committed. Had I written it today, it would have been worded differently."

Davis sighed. There was no point in accusing Fillmore of having jumped the gun, but Davis was sure the story would be counterproductive. It would generate an outpouring of "clues" from the lunatic fringe, that great body of citizens eager to get involved in a highly visible investigation just for the attention they would get. Nothing of real value would be discovered, and much time would be wasted.

"The story will keep our secretarial staff busy answering the phones," he said. "I hope they know how to screen out the crazies."

"We've had a few responses already," Fillmore said. "Mostly harmless lunatics. One or two good citizens, however, with pretty naive notions of what constitutes useful information. One lady thought the arm could be identified by the brand of artificial nails it had. She suggested taking it around to various beauty salons and showing it to their manicurists. She was sure someone would recognize it."

Davis chuckled, thinking of the uproar that would ensue if a detective suddenly thrust a human arm at an unsuspecting manicurist. "What did she say when you told her the arm had no artificial nails?"

"Said she couldn't imagine a woman in this day and age without them."

Chapter Three

Baxter Cawthon, chief executive officer of the Cawthon School of Burial Science, was not exactly the kind of person Davis and Fulford had thought he would be. Speculating on the man they were about to visit, they had envisioned a tall, gaunt, somber man with dark hair, a dark beard, soulful eyes ("What the hell are soulful eyes?" Davis had complained when Fulford made the observation), and the manner of an Episcopalian minister or Catholic priest.

Cawthon proved to be as far from that preconceived image as one could get. He was no more than five feet, six inches tall, rotund instead of lean, and beardless, with red hair that surrounded his head in an unruly mass. His face was disfigured by a lopsided, gargoyle-like grin. His demeanor was not solemn or magisterial. It was jovial.

Fulford looked at Davis with an expression that seemed to say, "What other surprises are in store for us?"

Davis was unable to respond to her inquiring glance because Cawthon had seized his hand and was pumping it vigorously, with no indication of letting go.

"I'm delighted to be of service to the police," he gushed, finally relinquishing Davis's hand. "I assume your visit doesn't reflect a professional interest in mortuary science."

Davis assured him that neither he nor his companion were at all interested in becoming undertakers. "We wish only to learn what happens to a body from the time it arrives in a mortuary until it is put in the grave."

"Well, you've come to the right place," Cawthon stated. "And at a good time, too. Our students have just begun work on a gentleman who died this morning. If you wish, you may watch how they ready him for the coffin."

He took them into a room that resembled the medical examiner's postmortem room.

At one side on a marble slab lay the body of a white, obese male, naked except for something that looked like a linen napkin draped over his genitals. A tube hanging from a reservoir of fluid had been, by means of a large needle, introduced into one of the arteries in his neck. A small electric pump pushed fluid from the reservoir down the tube into his body. Another tube coming from a thigh vein drained his blood into a canister.

"When a mortician receives a body," Cawthon explained, "he washes and disinfects the skin and hair. The eyes are closed, and usually caps are inserted behind the lids to prevent a sunken appearance. The facial muscles are molded into a pleasant expression, and an anticoagulant is injected into an artery so the blood remains fluid."

He stopped and looked at the two detectives inquiringly. "I'm sure all this sounds a bit gruesome to you. And it is. But with time one learns to accept it as a matter of course. The only time the procedure arouses any emotion in me is when the corpse is that of a young person, presumably robust and flourishing when alive, cut down in his or her prime. The corpse of a beautiful young woman is most affecting." He seemed consumed by genuine feeling. "Never again to be embraced, never again to be fondled or caressed. How tragic."

He pulled himself together with an apologetic smile and continued. Fulford's face showed her distaste for his emotional display.

"After the anticoagulant is administered, the body is injected with what we call arterial fluid, commonly called embalming fluid. That's what you see going on here." He gestured toward the corpse.

"Sometimes, as is the case when the body is obese, it is necessary to inject the abdominal region with cavity fluid to reach any areas not fully penetrated by the arterial fluid."

Davis and Fulford looked at one another with evident revulsion.

Cawthon went on, unabashed, "Often the facial features are wasted by illness or disfigured by accident, and we are obliged to repair the damage. We do this subdermally by injecting an appropriate amount of silicone. In cases where the face is mangled by trauma, we may have to create a mask to cover the area. All this is necessary to make the body suitable for viewing."

He stopped with an expectant look, almost as if he were an actor awaiting applause.

Davis had none to give. His eyes dwelt with morbid fascination on the spectacle before him as Cawthon's students, vinyl gloved and wearing face masks, adjusted the flow of arterial fluid into the man's body.

He felt his spirits sink to the bottom of the well. He looked at Leda Fulford, at her beautiful body, so vital and seemingly indestructible. His mind refused to imagine her, on some future day, lying on a cold stone slab, giving up her blood for some alien fluid.

Fulford, who also seemed depressed, said in a businesslike way, "Mr. Cawthon, do undertakers embalm every client they receive?"

"Most of the time relatives of the deceased want the body laid out for viewing. Embalming allows the mortician to neaten the body and, as I mentioned earlier, to restore the features when necessary. If a body is not to be viewed, it can be placed in a coffin immediately. I'd say about five percent of cases fall into that category. There is no law requiring embalming."

"So, embalmed or not, how long would a funeral director keep a body on his premises?"

"Two or three nights at the most. On rare occasions, it could be as long as a week. Some families want to delay interment until a distant relative can arrive for the services."

"If a body is not embalmed," Fulford paused, groping for an inoffensive way of putting the question, "and is kept for some time, wouldn't there be a problem of . . . odor?"

"Most undertakers have cold rooms, spaces where the temperature is kept in the low fifties or upper forties. At that level, decomposition is very slow."

Davis wanted to know about security measures. "Do morticians ever have instances of vandalism, attempts to desecrate bodies, things of that sort?"

"Rarely, but they do happen. Emotions run high at the time of bereavement. I remember one case. As the body of a local man lay on view in the mortuary chapel, he was attacked and stabbed by a woman he had jilted years before. A case of ritual murder after the fact, you might say."

"Don't you have security measures to prevent that sort of thing?"

"Indeed, we have. All kinds of locks, alarms, cameras, whatever. But they're all designed to protect the premises at night, and they do a good job of it. I've never heard of anyone breaking into a mortuary when the place was closed. It's quite another thing, however, to prevent some nut who's in the viewing line from falling on the corpse with a knife."

"What you're saying," said Fulford, "is that no one could get through a funeral home's security system successfully. Are you sure of that?"

"I don't see how it could be done." Cawthon paused thoughtfully. "From the kinds of questions you've been asking me, I assume you're investigating a case in which a dead body has disappeared, perhaps a grave robbery?"

"I see no reason why we shouldn't tell you what we're after," Davis said. "We've found the arm of an embalmed body and are trying to find out where it came from."

"And some cemetery operator told you it was impossible to rob one of his graves. Right?"

"Words to that effect, yes," Fulford said.

"Ha!" Cawthon said derisively. "Grave robbing has an ancient and dishonorable history. The medical profession at one time had to depend on stolen bodies for the study of human anatomy because religious and societal attitudes kept people from allowing bodies to be used for instructional purposes. The resultant shortage created a lucrative trade in bodies stolen from graves. Families of newly buried persons used to stand guard for days or weeks at the grave site until the body of their loved one became unfit for dissection purposes.

"In some cities like Edinburgh, where there was a large medical school, and where grave robbing was difficult, some unsavory types took to murdering vagrants to supply the demand."

"That's all very interesting," said Davis. "But conditions seem to have changed. Grave robbing these days is almost impossible."

"Who told you it was? Did you speak with Fenwick Cooper of Willow Rest by any chance?"

"Yes."

"I thought as much. He didn't tell you, I'm sure, that the elaborate security measures at Willow Rest were installed after the body of a state supreme court justice was disinterred there and hung from an oak tree, presumably by a disgruntled victim of the judge's judicial wrath. This happened about five years ago and resulted in a great improvement in cemetery security systems, especially at Willow Rest. But not all cemeteries were able, financially, to beef up security to the degree Willow Rest did. Fenwick is probably right about his place. It would be mighty tough to rob one of his graves, but there are lots of small cemeteries in the region without the safety measures Willow Rest has."

"So," Davis said, "one of their graves could easily be robbed?"

"I wouldn't say easily, but if carefully planned, it could be done, and probably without detection."

Davis listened to this statement with dismay. He had little enthusiasm for visiting a dozen or more small cemeteries, hoping to find one that had, or that would admit to having had, a recent grave robbery. But if Cawthon's belief was correct, that stealing a body from a large cemetery or from a mortuary was next to impossible, he would have no alternative.

"Can you tell me," he asked Cawthon, "of any cemeteries you think might be vulnerable to theft?"

"A lot of small cemeteries are ethnic ones. You can rule out the black ones since the arm you have is that of a white woman. You might also exclude places that cater to other minorities that wouldn't fit your description. I'll get up a list of likely places for you if you like."

"We'd appreciate it," Fulford said. "And thank you for your cooperation."

As they turned to go, they saw Cawthon's students inserting a long needle into the abdomen of the fat man's corpse. The detectives pulled their eyes away from the spectacle and returned hurriedly to the busy streets of central Atlanta, where throngs of people swirled and life pulsated.

"Congestion," Davis said, "may be one of the great nuisances of modern life. But after that little session with the dead, I love it."

It was ten-thirty, and Davis and Fulford decided it was time for a coffee break. They found a diner and sat in a corner booth, sipping a house specialty, mocha walnut. Davis made a face.

"Coffee used to be coffee," he said. "Period. Now it's got to be some crazy mixture of dry-roasted beans and something like butterscotch. You ever tasted butterscotch coffee?"

"No," she said. "And you never did either."

"Well, it's in the realm of possibility, isn't it? I'll take good old-fashioned coffee any day to this stuff."

"I'll tell you a secret," Fulford confided, in the manner of a spy disclosing classified material. "If you put enough sugar and cream in it, you can't tell it from the real thing."

He followed her advice and found the cup tolerable.

"Speaking of the real thing, where do we go from here? I don't relish digging into the premises of the dead, if you'll pardon the horrible pun. By the way, what's a little cemetery? One with twenty graves, a hundred, two hundred?"

"Cemeteries are probably measured in acres," Fulford replied. "A small one might have three or four acres."

"And how many bodies can you cram into an acre?" Davis asked with evident distaste. He made a gesture of revulsion. "I'm sick of dogging the dear departed. It's giving me the creeps. I'm ready for another approach."

"Looking for cemetery vandals is like plumbing a dry well," Fulford said. "So far it's got us nowhere, and I don't think it will get us anywhere in the future. Let's go back to the beginning. When McAllister found the arm, it was weighted down with something called came. So whoever threw it in the Chattahoochee had to have access to the stuff. Not many people would."

"You're right. Only someone working with stained glass—making windows, for instance—would have a supply of it. Shouldn't be too hard to get a line on that kind of person. He or she would have to buy the came from a wholesaler, or if wholesalers don't sell retail, he'd have to buy it from a hobby shop or a crafts store."

As they drove back to headquarters, Davis said, "Want to look in the yellow pages again, Leda? See if you can find a came distributor. If you can't find one, try locating a few hobby stores, preferably ones on the west side, close to the Chattahoochee. I'm assuming the person who tossed the arm lived close to the river."

"Which might not be true," Fulford said. "He, if it is a he, could have carried the arm across Atlanta, or the whole state of Georgia, for that matter, on a car seat beside him."

"True, but closer seems more likely. Let's start with places near the river and work outward."

"No problem, boss," she said.

He looked at her attractive profile, congratulating himself on the good fortune that had placed them together.

"I'm not your boss," he said. "I'm your colleague. Colleagues are equal."

"In the abstract," she said playfully. "On the job, maybe not. Who always gets sent to the yellow pages?"

"I asked nicely, didn't I? Tell you what," he said, as if grievously wounded by her charge, "I'll help you turn the pages."

She laughed. "Big deal. I'm overwhelmed."

The next morning, neither of them had to resort to the yellow pages. A note on Davis's desk listed Marygold McAllister's phone number and asked him to return her call.

"She's the one who brought you that wretched arm in the first place, isn't she?" Fulford said. "I wonder what she wants?"

"Let's find out." Davis listened as McAllister's phone rang. "I hope she hasn't found any more body parts."

"I heard that remark," McAllister said. "No, I haven't found any more body parts. My luck ran out, I guess. I'm speaking to Detective Davis, I presume?"

"You are, and I'm pleased to hear from you. I'm guessing you've got some information for me."

"I hope you find it useful. When I saw the story in the paper about your seeking help from the public, I thought of something. Perfectly obvious thing. I'm sure you've thought of it. If you could find a person or persons who had came in their possession, you might be on to a possible culprit. Not everyone would have a strip of came available to weigh down an arm, would they?"

"No, they wouldn't, and yes, we've thought of conducting a search for such a person."

"Well, maybe I can help speed your task. I know that came is sold only in crafts stores or in shops that make a specialty of doing leaded glass. I can think of two places you might want to visit. There's Bernhardt's Glass on Fulton Industrial Boulevard. They sell colored glass, came, and copper foil, and they also make windows and glass doors to order. Maybe they could supply you with a list of customers to whom they sell came.

"Then there's Art's Crafts—cute, huh?—near Collier, close to where it runs into Lincoln Park Memorial Cemetery.

"Neither of these places is far from the Chattahoochee, where I fished up the arm. I don't know whether that's important or not, but I think it makes good sense to start looking there before looking farther away, don't you?"

"I do," said Davis. "We're indebted to you, Ms. McAllister, for your cooperation. Your suggestions are most helpful. I promise again to keep you posted on the investigation."

She gave a short laugh. "I don't think I'll wait for you to call me. Why don't I call you?"

Davis hung up the phone. "Marygold McAllister, bless her soul, has just given us a couple of hot leads."

He told her of Bernhardt's Glass and Art's Crafts.

She smiled at Art's sophomoric wit and said, "Let's tackle Art first. He sounds like a towering intellect."

Art's Crafts was a modest establishment, cluttered with an assortment of model ships and pre-cut birdhouse kits, racks of oil and acrylic paint tubes, cases of artist's paintbrushes, hanks of multicolored yarn, rows of needlepoint canvases, and troughs filled with came. Art, the proprietor, exuded geniality. He came beaming toward them like the maitre d' of an expensive restaurant. When he was informed that Davis and Fulford were homicide detectives there on official business, business they did not disclose to him, he dropped his occupational cordiality and answered their questions matter-of-factly.

"Yes, I have several customers who buy came regularly. Most of them buy only four or five strips at a time."

"How long is a strip?"

"Six feet."

Davis exchanged knowing glances with Fulford. The strip of came wound around McAllister's trophy catch was exactly six feet.

"That's interesting," Davis said. "Is it sold in different sizes or gauges?"

"It is. I stock one-eighth and three-eighth gauges. I don't have any customers doing real heavy work requiring a larger gauge."

"You said most of your customers buy only small amounts," Fulford said. "Does that mean you have some who buy large quantities?"

"I had in mind one particular customer. He makes decorative panels of colored glass. Flowers, animals, birds, things like that. Right now he's into egrets and peacocks. Very pretty. He exhibits and sells at crafts shows, county fairs, and art galleries."

"What gauge does he buy?" Davis was plumbing his memory for the size of the came that encircled the dismembered arm.

"I think one-eighth. The stuff he makes is small. He uses a lot of copper foil, too."

"What's copper foil?"

"It's a thin sheet of copper that can be molded around the edges of a piece of glass. Two pieces of a pattern with foil on their edges can be put together and soldered. The joint is weaker than a came joint, but finer and neater looking."

"Who is this fellow?" Davis asked.

"Name's Ralph Hamlet." He consulted a file. "Lives at twelve twenty-five Wisteria Way in Kirkwood. I think he's a professor at some college, in chemistry or biological sciences. Something like that."

"You have any customers who live on the west side of town near the Chattahoochee?" Fulford asked.

"Let me look." He searched through the file again and gave her an affirmative nod. "Yes. There's one. A lady who lives on Sandy Creek Road, near Nixon Park. Name of Marygold McAllister."

"You call her," Davis said. "I'll listen in. Pretend you just learned she was the one who brought in the arm. Then surprise her with what Art told us. We'll see how she reacts."

Fulford pressed McAllister's number and heard a voice say, "Marygold McAllister here."

"Ms. McAllister, I'm Detective Leda Fulford of Homicide Division. I'm calling about the severed arm you recently discovered."

"Very nice of you to keep in touch. Have you learned anything new?"

"As a matter of fact, we have." Fulford paused for dramatic impact. "We are told by Art of Art's Crafts that you buy came from him regularly."

There was silence. After a lengthy pause, McAllister said, "That's true. I make decorative panels for Christmas gifts and for birthdays and special occasions. There was another pause. "I assume you're busy drawing incriminating inferences from that fact."

"Such inferences are almost inescapable," Fulford said.

"I suppose they are, though I thought Detective Davis might have considered me above suspicion. It's a blow to my self-esteem. Let me see if I can duplicate his and your thinking. A woman appears in his office bearing a severed arm wrapped in a strip of came. She claims to have caught the arm while fishing in the Chattahoochee. Possibly she did. But her story may be a hoax. For reasons unknown, she, having came at her disposal, wrapped it around the arm and pretended to have found it in the river. Isn't that the way he's thinking?"

Davis, who had been listening with fascination, spoke up, "When you laid that arm on my desk, Ms. McAllister, you spoke knowledgeably about came and its uses. Why didn't you tell me your knowledge was from having used it yourself?"

"Had you asked me, I would have done so. The fact that I've used came and have some in my possession doesn't mean I had anything to do with that arm. I can't think of any reason whatsoever for my being crazy enough to wrap up an embalmed arm with came and pretend I found it in the river. Tell me, can you offer one sensible reason for my having done that?"

Davis spoke reluctantly, "At the moment, I can't. But perhaps I'm hampered by thinking rationally."

"Thanks," McAllister said with a sarcastic laugh. "Do you really think I'm a lunatic?"

"No, I don't think you're crazy. Even if I did, I'd have trouble figuring out how you could have gotten hold of the arm."

At Bernhardt's Glass, they were met by an attractive blonde woman, probably in her late forties, who wore a white smock over her shirt and jeans. She also wore a broad, amiable smile and an aspect of dynamic energy.

"Are you the proprietor?" Davis asked.

"I am. Sarah Bernhardt, no less."

Davis noted the name. "Do people ever mention you're named for a famous actress?"

"Actually, few people ever make the connection. I certainly didn't expect it from a couple of cops."

She flushed in embarrassment at the unintended derogation. "I mean," she stammered, "one doesn't think of theater being a part of police academy training."

"It's not," Davis replied without resentment. "It's something Detective Fulford and I have picked up on the side."

"I hope you're not offended."

"Not in the least. We're here investigating the case of a missing person. We believe someone who works with came or has it readily at hand may have knowledge that could help us. What we'd like to know is if you have any customers who buy came from you."

"We don't sell came retail," Bernhardt said. "We wholesale to hobby and crafts shops and to one or two glass shops whose business it is to make colored glass things for retail sale.

"In fact, the sale of came is only a small part of our business. We make and sell fancy windows and doors mostly. We do make a number of small glass objects like tissue boxes, framed mirrors, and decorative panels."

She gestured to the objects surrounding them. They were standing in what served as a showroom. Set up in frames were several heavy oak doors with colorful leaded glass panels installed where opaque wooden panels normally would have been. Other doors were fitted with panels of clear beveled glass that glowed like jewels in the refracted light. Several windows with Tiffany-like forest scenes were hung where light from the rear illuminated their colors. Tucked away on shelves and in niches were jewelry and tissue boxes, ashtrays, and soap dishes.

"These things are beautiful," Fulford said. "You can't do all of this yourself. You must have quite a crew of workers."

"We're actually like a small factory. I employ four people, three women and one man, all of whom have a knack for cutting glass and a good eye for color combinations and artistic patterns. Come back into our workroom and see how we build things."

The workroom, the size of a small warehouse, held four long tables on which glass was being assembled. A single smaller table served as a workbench for the construction of three-dimensional artifacts—two tissue boxes and a strikingly beautiful jewelry box.

On one side of the room, a sturdy rack held panes of glass standing on edge at a slight angle so one could flip through them by moving each pane a few inches to the right or left. Next to the glass were several rows of troughs that held strips of came.

Sarah Bernhardt introduced them to her crew. They were Fran Tanner, a slight, muscular woman with a cherub's face; Kristin Corum, a blond, Scandinavian-looking, full-bosomed girl of jovial disposition; Molly Meldrum, terribly shy, embarrassed at meeting them, whose blotched, acne-scarred face was the source of her distress, Davis assumed; and, finally, Donovan Grey. Almost as big as Davis, Grey looked at them with childlike interest, but there was a vacuity about his expression that puzzled Davis.

After looking Fulford up and down in a sensual way, Grey said, "You're a pretty girl. I like pretty girls. Do you like me?"

Before Fulford could recover from her surprise, Sarah Bernhardt placed her hand on Grey's shoulder and said, "Now, Donnie, remember your manners. Be nice."

Grey flushed and turned away.

"Let's all go back to work," Bernhardt said, and the four retreated to their respective work tables.

A few minutes later, Davis and Fulford were seated in Bernhardt's office.

"I try to hire the handicapped where possible," Bernhardt said. "Molly Meldrum is emotionally scarred from being brutalized as a child and from the blemishes on her face. She needs a quiet, semi-isolated place in which to work. Confronting strangers, as you observed, is very painful for her."

"I felt so sorry for her," Fulford said.

"She does well here," Bernhardt said. "She's skilled with her hands, uses a soldering iron beautifully, and works diligently.

"Donovan Grey is something else again. You may have sensed he's retarded. He has the mind of an eight- or ten-year-old and the directness and candor, as you can appreciate, Ms. Fulford, of a child. But he has an amazing sense of pattern and color harmony. He's designed some of the windows we've been commissioned to build. There's a small, privately-owned museum in Marietta devoted to shoes, of all things, throughout the ages. They asked for two windows that exemplified the shoemaker's art. I asked Donnie to have a go at it. What he designed was absolutely astonishing. The museum director couldn't praise the work highly enough.

"A few years ago he might have been called an idiot-savant. Now it's proper to say he's intellectually challenged."

"Has his penchant for coming on to attractive women ever caused trouble?"

"Not really. Some female customers are taken aback at his frankness, but they quickly perceive his limitations and make allowances for it."

"He eyed Detective Fulford in a pretty sexual way," Davis said. "Aren't you afraid he may someday get out of hand?"

"I've thought about it, but I don't think Donnie would know what to do with a woman, sexually, that is, if he ever had the opportunity. He's of the age, emotionally, when boys satisfy their sexual urges by masturbating. I would guess Donnie relieves himself in that way."

Fulford had a questioning look on her face, as if she didn't totally trust Bernhardt's response. Donnie might have the mental age of a ten-year-old, she thought, but he has the body of an adult male. Why not an adult male's sexual behavior? She decided not to press the matter, however.

"Where does he live?" she asked.

"Somewhere in Corey Park with his mother."

"Corey Park's on the west side, isn't it? Not too far from the Chattahoochee?"

"That's right. He takes the bus to work, but if the weather's bad, his mother drives him. She seems devoted to him. When he first started working for me, she invited me to dinner to discuss Donnie's 'problem.' When Donnie left the room after our meal, she spoke frankly about the need for me, as his employer, to understand and allow for his limitations. She is realistic about his abilities. She wants him to be as independent as possible but knows that without her, unless she provides for him otherwise, he would have to be institutionalized. She has made arrangements with a young couple to become his foster parents upon her death. She has set up a trust fund for that purpose."

She paused, reflecting. "Maybe you ought to talk to Donnie's mother yourselves. She can tell you much more about him than I can."

Davis considered that possibility. He wanted to know more about Donovan's limitations, especially more about his sexual behavior. But the time was not right.

He shook his head. "I don't want to do that. At least, not right now. We don't suspect Donnie of having anything to do with the missing person we're hunting for. We're just gathering information that might be of use to us. We would be grateful for anything else you can tell us about Donnie."

"There is one more thing," she said hesitantly. "Of a delicate nature. I refer to Donnie's sexual needs, about which you are rightfully concerned. I told you earlier I thought he satisfied his needs by masturbating, and you, Ms. Fulford, seemed to have some reservations. That idea was more than a surmise on my part based on his mental age and emotional development. I got the idea from Donnie's mother, who, I believe, has consulted family counselors.

"Parents of mentally challenged children have to confront the problem brought on by their children's sexual development. When the child is female, some parents have her sterilized. It's a simple matter to have the Fallopian tubes tied. The girl is thus spared the prospect of becoming pregnant if she manages to have intercourse."

"But Donnie's not a girl," Fulford said. "He could have a vasectomy, but I don't see what good that would do. His sex drive would be undiminished. He still might become dangerously aggressive toward women."

"That's true, and in order to lessen that possibility, I believe his mother has encouraged him to masturbate. I told you earlier that, when he first started to work for me, I had dinner with her and Donnie. When Donnie had gone to bed, Mrs. Grey went into the kitchen to make some tea. I took the liberty of scanning her bookshelves. I spotted a volume, written in simple language, about autoeroticism. It was called *Love Alone and Like It*, and it was there for Donnie to read, I'm sure."

Neither Davis nor Fulford doubted her assumption.

Davis said, "I confess, I never realized the problem sexual development creates in cases like Donnie's. I suppose Mrs. Grey's method of dealing with it is as good as any. I don't know what else she could do."

"Maybe Mrs. Grey could get Donnie interested in some kind of physical activity, like athletics, to drain off some of his energy," Fulford said.

"She's enrolled him in a fitness club where he works out daily," Bernhardt said, "and she encourages him to take on other activities. He's become an enthusiastic bird-watcher, goes out weekends with binoculars and a notebook to record his sightings. She told me he has seen some birds considered rare in this area. Last summer he spotted a mourning warbler and a Connecticut warbler. Sighting rarities such as those gives him great satisfaction."

"Does he belong to a bird club?"

"I don't think so. With him it's a solitary activity. His mother drives him out to the woods someplace and comes back to pick him up in an hour or two. Sometimes he goes by bus."

She sat for a moment, a thoughtful expression on her face. Then, looking at the detectives, she said, "I can think of nothing more about Donnie, or any of my employees, that might be of interest to you. Fran Tanner and Kirsten Corum are both married and are solid citizens, as far as I can tell."

Davis and Fulford rose, thanked her, and left.

The next morning, Fulford said to Davis, "I wonder if Donnie Grey might have had something to do with that severed arm. He certainly had access to all the came he needed."

She paused, an uncertain expression on her face.

"Only trouble is," she added, "what possible motive could he have had?"

"And," Davis said, "if we assume Donnie threw the arm into the Chattahoochee, where would he have gotten it, except from the body? Do you think Donnie has hidden a body away somewhere? Seems far-fetched to me."

While they were speculating on the possible culpability of Donovan Grey, a messenger came by and dropped a packet of letters on Davis's desk. He handed another packet to Fulford. Both skimmed through the envelopes. Davis cast his aside after finding nothing interesting or imperative.

Fulford was about to do the same when her eye was caught by an envelope, addressed in crude, block letters: DETECTIVE FULFORD, HOMICIDE, ATLANTA POLICE. No street number, no zip code, and no return address were given. She opened the envelop carefully, withdrew a single sheet, and read a message which, like the address, was written in hand-printed block letters.

WANT TO FIND THE REST OF HER?
TAKE A GAMBLE
IF YOU THINK IN PAIRS
YOU'LL LEARN THE PLACE
HER BODY SHARES.

She handed the sheet to Davis. "What do you make of this?"

He studied the message briefly, turned it over, examined the back side, and inspected the envelope. "I'd be inclined to think it's a hoax, except it's addressed to you."

"What difference does that make?"

"The story Gerry put in the newspaper gave my name as the officer to contact for persons having information about the case. Since this message is directed to you, it had to come from a person who knew you were working on the case with me."

"Of course," Fulford said. "That means it could not have come from Fenwick Cooper, or any other cemetery administrator, because you talked to them by phone. They had no inkling I was involved."

"But Baxter Cawthon and his crew of students knew. Five of them, weren't there?" Davis said. "And so did Sarah Bernhardt and her employees."

"Don't forget Art Walker of Art's Crafts."

"For some reason, I don't see Art doing something like this. I'd put him at the bottom of the list."

He paused, trying to gauge whether it would be useful, at that particular moment, to try to discover the author of the note.

"Let's not worry right now about who sent the note," he said. "I think whoever sent it is trying, in this odd way, to tell us where the body is located. So let's see if we can solve the riddle." He stared intently at the note. "We're told that by thinking in pairs we'll find a clue to the location of the body. What kind of pairs is the writer talking about?"

"I can think of lots of pairs," Fulford said, "but they don't seem very helpful. Things like night and day, short and tall, sweet and sour, black and white. What good are they?"

"Not much. I was on a slightly different track, thinking of complementary pairs like love and marriage, horse and carriage, stuff like that." He paused, concentrating. "We're not going at it right, Leda. We could dredge up hundreds of pairs like that, and none of them would point to anything. But the writer of the note meant for us to discover a pair that would tell us where to look for the body."

"Exactly. So we have to think of pairs that are associated with a place, a location of some sort."

"Like what?" Davis asked.

"I'm having trouble thinking of an example." Lines of intense thought furrowed her brow. "This is not very good," she said after several moments, "but it's the best I can do right off the top of my head. Take two people, Jessica Tandy and Hume Cronin. When you hear those two names, what do you think of?"

"The movies, the theater."

"So if the writer wanted to tell us the body was hidden in a theater, he might have a pair like that in mind."

"Okay. I get your point. Unfortunately, how would we ever think of the right pair? And if we did, how would we ever know if it was the right one?"

"So the author had to make sure, somehow, we'd eventually come up with the right pair."

"He was forced to put a clue in the message itself so we'd know when we hit upon the thing he had in mind. Agreed?"

As they sat in Benson's Pizza Parlor lunching on Benson's latest pizza innovation, the Square Deal, Davis lectured Fulford on the superiority, from a gastronomic point of view, of the square pizza over the round one.

"With the Square Deal, the customer gets more to eat. In a round pizza, the corners are cut off. I'd guess perhaps two-fifths of a round pizza are lost when the corners are lopped off."

"You amaze me, Wade," Fulford said. "Anyone who could figure that out ought to have no trouble working out the meaning of this simple, cryptic message."

"Do I detect a trace of sarcasm in that remark? I promise you I'll get to the bottom of this puzzle if it's the last thing I do."

"What's the last thing you're going to do?" a voice interrupted them.

They looked up. The voice belonged to Albert Saffron, an overweight giant of a man, a colleague in the Homicide Division who, a couple of years earlier, had beaten back an attempt by management to have him fired because of his bulk. With the help of a couple of lawyers from the American Civil Liberties Union, he created a new category of persons entitled to protection under the Americans with Disabilities Act: the obese.

Davis had been one of his staunchest supporters, and the two had become great friends. Davis had grown accustomed to needling Saffron by good-natured references to his bulk.

"Albert, sit down," he said. "But gently. We don't want you to set off the Richter scale."

Albert, used to jokes aimed at his ponderous body, smiled at Davis's remark and responded with a jibe at his friend's expense. "For a man with a limited imagination," he replied, "that was clever in a childish way." He looked narrowly at the two. "Judging from your worried expressions, you're blundering through this found-arm case, stumbling into barriers, and running off in all directions."

Davis, remembering previous times when Albert had steered him into alternative and rewarding interpretations of evidence, readily acknowledged his perplexity.

"As a matter of fact," Davis said, "we're trying to make sense of this note." He handed it to Albert.

Albert studied the note carefully as he chewed huge bites of pizza.

"Well," he said, "it's obvious, isn't it?" He paused, looking at his two companions with an expression of exaggerated pity.

"Not to us," Davis said.

"I fear," Albert said, "you are unable to see the trees because of the forest. Or is it the other way around?"

"Spare us the adages," Fulford said. "One enigma is all I can take at this point."

"Okay," Albert replied. "The writer of this note gave you half of the solution to the puzzle. He had to. You would never come up with the right pair unless he did. Look at the message and find a word that could be part of a pair."

"All right," Davis said. He ran his eye over the message a word at a time. "What about gamble?"

"Sounds possible. What would pair with gamble?"

"I can think of a dozen possibilities," Fulford said. "Like dice, and lotto, and blackjack."

"And risk, and odds, and chance," Davis offered, aware that none of the words he and Fulford had offered made much sense.

"We've been using common nouns," said Albert, "and common nouns are getting us nowhere."

"So we try proper nouns," Davis said. "Let's give it a whirl."

Fulford, who had been peering at the note with enormous concentration, suddenly called out, "Got it. It's Procter, as in 'Procter and Gamble,' the soap people. That has to be it. Procter would point us to Proctor Creek. Our anonymous author is telling us the body is somewhere in the region of the creek. Proctor Creek runs into the Chattahoochee just north of Bankhead Bridge, not far from where the arm was found."

Davis looked at Albert with genuine affection. "Albert, you're a genius. Without you to nudge us in the right direction, God knows how many hours we would have spent on that riddle. Remind me to buy you a beer someday."

"Ha!" Albert said. "Given your past record of generosity, I'd better rely on my own resources for liquid refreshment."

"I think," Davis said, as his crew unloaded a flat-bottomed boat from the pickup, "the body is probably at the bottom of one of the creek's deeper pools, weighted down, most likely, with came, like the arm McAllister fished up was. Let's begin at the mouth and move upstream, working the bottom of every pool big enough to hide a body."

A patrolman fastened a trolling motor to the rear of the boat, and the four—two patrolmen, Davis, and Fulford—began moving upstream, peering into the murky water, and scraping their grapple-hooked poles across the bottom whenever they saw a potential hiding place.

Davis found it uncanny work. The stream was narrow enough to be, in places, canopied over with huge water oaks. Their outstretched limbs, drooping with Spanish moss, seemed as if they were about to enfold the searchers in a deadly embrace. He shook off the feeling of dread and said to Fulford, "I've done more agreeable things in my time."

"My feeling exactly," Fulford replied. "I hope we're not misreading that note."

About two miles upstream, the water became so shallow it could no longer conceal a body, and they turned the boat around, facing downstream.

"What now?" Fulford asked.

"It seems," Davis said, "we made a bum guess when we assumed the perpetrator hid the body in the water. He's either buried it or concealed it in some other way along the banks. Let's drift back downstream, keeping our eyes out for any sign of her."

"I hope we spot her," Fulford said. "I don't relish the prospect of exploring both sides of the stream for a fresh grave."

The boat drifted slowly. Four pairs of eyes scanned the banks with rigorous scrutiny. The boat was not more than a hundred yards from the Chattahoochee when they found the body.

It lay beneath a willow tree whose branches hung to the ground, a curtain of green lace drawn across a melancholy scene. Except for a fortunate gap in the foliage, through which they caught a quick glimpse of an indistinct figure, they would never have seen her as they drifted by.

Approaching her resting place by land, they encountered a thicket of berry bushes that formed a thorny barrier, shutting out the light and impeding entry into the bower beneath the tree. When they at last forced their way in, they saw the forlorn naked body of a young woman lying face up, her white skin barely visible in the dim light; she seemed asleep, as though she were still infused with the life that had been taken from her.

"What a pretty thing she was," Fulford said as she stood looking at the pathetic, doll-like remnant of what was once a living person. "What a shame she had to die."

Davis tried to suppress the bitter memory that rose in his mind but could not. Once again, with appalling reality, he relived the dreadful scene. The semi-truck careening across the median, the grinding of twisting metal, the showering of broken glass, the swift passage into oblivion. The horrible realization, when he returned to consciousness, that he was unhurt, save for minor cuts and bruises, but that his wife, Sylvia, lying on the shoulder of the road where medics had placed her, was shattered beyond recovery. It had taken years to obliterate that memory. Now, as he saw the naked, dead body before him, the memory was back.

He felt depressed and angry.

"Get used to it, Leda," he said. "Cops have to face one outrage after another in the course of a day's work."

"I doubt I'll ever get used to it," she replied.

Davis turned to one of the patrolmen. "String up some tape and stay with her until the medical examiner and the crime scene people arrive," he said.

He and Fulford drove silently back to headquarters.

Davis took from the file the envelope and note that had led to the discovery of the body and handed them across the desk to Fulford. "The postmark doesn't help us any," he said. "It was mailed at the biggest substation on the north side. The station serves hundreds of thousands of people. And the envelope is the kind you can buy in any drugstore or any discount mart. No help there."

He paused briefly.

"But look at the paper the note is written on. See anything unusual about it?"

"Yes, I do. I don't know what it's called—tracing paper, maybe—but it's parchment-like and semitransparent. And it seems to be cut from a larger sheet."

"Exactly," Davis replied. "And I wonder if you remember where we've seen paper like it."

"In Sarah Bernhardt's glass factory."

"Unless we're mistaken. But anyone making a stained glass window would use that kind of paper, not just Bernhardt's crew. Art Walker tells me it's called pattern paper. A glass worker draws the pattern of a window on this kind of paper, tacks it to a workbench, cuts the pieces of the glass to fit, and lays them on the pattern where he or she can join them together with came."

"So anyone might have a supply of it, not just Bernhardt's."

"Right. But whoever sent the message was not just anyone. He or she had to know about the arm and about our appeal for help concerning it. But most important, the writer had to know where the body was hidden. I'm willing to bet a month's salary the note came from someone in Bernhardt's establishment. Perhaps from Sarah herself."

"Or Donovan Grey," Fulford said.

Davis nodded. He knew it was unjust to suspect Grey simply because he was retarded, but just or not, Donnie had to be considered. He wondered, for instance, if Grey's lack of emotional development could diminish the inhibitions that ordinarily deter people from crime.

Fulford appeared dubious. "I don't think Donnie could have written that note. It's a bit too clever for him."

"Don't be so sure," Davis said. "I've heard of intellectually challenged children who are math whizzes. Donnie may have as much genius for word games as he has for pattern and color harmony. And don't forget, he's a bird-watcher. Tramps around in the wilderness with binoculars. Who would be more likely to spot a dead body?"

"I take it then," Fulford said, "we're obliged to pay another visit to Bernhardt and her crew."

"As soon as we see what Chris can tell us about the body."

"What the hell am I supposed to do with a dead, embalmed body?" complained McCalmon when they confronted him. "Do an autopsy to find out what killed her? Tell you if she's been raped? Check to see if she's HIV positive?"

"Simmer down, Chris," Davis said. "I'm sure you've given her a preliminary examination. Tell us if you found anything unusual."

"Well, her arm's been cut off. And the arm McAllister fished out of the Chattahoochee fits her perfectly. Probably the two of you would have noticed those things without my help."

"Spare us the sarcasm," Fulford said. She liked Chris, especially his ability to handle human remains with dignity and a surprising tenderness. His irreverence, as she had surmised the first time she met him, seemed not disrespectful, but merely a way of coping with the most repellent aspects of human life. He was young and handsome, too, and had a refreshing directness. She pressed him for information, adopting a flirtatious manner.

"Come on, handsome. Any idea how long she's been dead?"

Chris, captivated, responded readily, "I'd say not long. No longer than several months. An embalmed body shows certain signs of age that she doesn't yet exhibit. Her eyes, after I removed the caps, have sunk very little; her flesh is firm, unmarked by mold or desiccation. All in all, I'd say she's in pretty good shape, a tribute to the guy who embalmed her."

"Any marks on her," Davis asked, "that might give a clue to who she is? Can you tell if she's been removed from a casket?"

"The answer to the first question is no. There are no birthmarks, no signs of old fractures or recent injuries. She even has perfect teeth. Not a single cavity. If she had once been in a casket, we might find threads of fabric stuck to her clothes. But she's naked. There's nothing clinging to her skin."

"Well," said Davis, "when you have time, could you have a look at her internal organs?"

"What the devil for? What do you expect to learn from the viscera of an embalmed body?"

"Maybe nothing, but there's a chance you might find traces of a few common poisons."

"Fat chance. For most poisons we'd need blood samples. She hasn't got any blood, remember?"

"Some poisons like arsenic leave traces in the tissues, don't they? Aren't there other poisons that leave traces like arsenic?"

"Hell, Wade, off the top of my head, I can't think of any. I'd have to research it."

"What about a ruptured spleen or a liver damaged by hepatitis? Things like that."

"What you're asking will take hours. How much time do you expect me to spend on this body? I've got other things to do. And what good would it do you if I did determine a probable cause of death?"

"I don't know," Davis admitted. "It might point us in one direction or another."

Fulford, looking disgusted, said, "Come on, you two. Let's quit arguing. Aren't we ready to go, Wade?"

"Don't go, Leda," Chris implored. "I'll die if you leave me."

"I'll bet!" She made a face at him. "I'll check in tomorrow to see if you're still alive."

Chapter Four

"Yes," Sarah Bernhardt said, "that's the kind of paper we use, and yes, you're correct in assuming it wouldn't be marketed in pieces that small. Our paper comes in rolls, thirty-six inches wide. Like yard goods in a fabric store."

"So it could have come from your stock?" Davis asked.

"It could have, but it could have come from dozens of other sources, too. Everyone in this business uses it."

Fulford shifted the inquiry abruptly. "Do you ever do any fishing, any hiking, any kind of outdoor activity?"

Bernhardt laughed. "My feet are wedded to asphalt and concrete. They get uneasy when I walk across my lawn."

Fulford smiled at her locution. "What about some of your help? Molly Meldrum, for instance. You told us she's a recluse. Fishing and hiking are solitary activities."

"As far as I know, she's not a wilderness person," Bernhardt said. "She spends her time reading. Reading can be the most solitary activity of all, can't it?"

Davis nodded. He remembered how he had buried himself in books after his wife's death. He had been, for many months, a fugitive from reality, a closeted bibliophile, hiding between the covers of one book after another.

"How about Donovan Grey?" Fulford asked. "You told us he was an avid bird-watcher. Bird-watchers spend a lot of time in the woods, right?"

Bernhardt looked at the detectives with a puzzled expression. "I don't understand your line of questioning. Why so much interest in folks who love the great outdoors?"

Fulford looked at Davis, a question in her expression. He shrugged in a permissive way.

"A minute ago we showed you a piece of paper," she said,

"showed you the reverse side because we didn't want you to see the message that was written on the front. The message told us where we would find the body of a dead woman."

"I gather," interrupted Bernhardt, "you found the body somewhere in a wooded area. Hence, the odd questions."

"Yes," Davis said. "We thought it only logical that the writer of the note was a person who loved the great outdoors, as you put it. Someone who spent a lot of time in the woods." He looked at her expectantly.

Bernhardt frowned. She seemed reluctant to express the thought that hovered in everyone's mind. "The only person who comes close to meeting your criterion," she said, "is Donovan Grey."

"I think we'd better talk to him," Davis said. "Is he here?"

"He's here," said Bernhardt, "but . . ." She seemed uncertain and determined at the same time. As she spoke, she looked Davis squarely in the eye, as if daring him to disagree with her. "I'm afraid I can't allow you to question him on my premises." She paused uncertainly, as if an explanation were called for. "He's an innocent. If he's to be questioned, he needs an advocate, someone to make sure he understands what's at stake. Someone to shield him from abuse."

Fulford bridled a bit. "It's not our intention to abuse him, Mrs. Bernhardt. A few questions will tell us if he's the one who wrote the note."

"And it was not my intention to offend you," retorted Bernhardt. "Surely you agree that it will be much better if his mother is present when he's questioned."

Davis said soothingly, "You're quite right. We'll handle this in a proper way. He can even have a lawyer present, if his mother chooses, though he is not being accused of a crime."

They ended their conversation with Bernhardt in a cool and formal fashion

Mrs. Grey was upset. When Davis suggested she might want a lawyer, she emphatically denied the need for such a person. Her resentment and apprehension at the proceeding, however, were evident.

"What do you suspect Donnie of?" she asked. "I can't imagine he's done anything bad, anything illegal. I hope you don't suspect him because he's 'different.' That would be unfair."

"No, ma'am," Davis said. "We've been told that in some ways

he's not ordinary, but that has nothing to do with our inquiry."

"Donnie's problem is definitely not ordinary," Mrs. Grey said. She seemed determined to see that the detectives knew all about her son before they questioned him. "I've taken him to several clinics, had him examined by medical experts, taken him to psychiatrists. He does not fit any preconceived model. He's not autistic, he does not suffer from Down's syndrome, he has not had a birth injury. What seems to have happened to Donnie is that most of his intellectual development stopped when he was in the fifth grade. He performs at a high level in some areas, like spatial skills and verbal conundrums, but otherwise he's—I hate to use the word—retarded."

She paused with a diffident expression. "You must excuse a mother's garrulity. I think you may find it understandable." She then assumed a self-conscious formality. "What's all this about a body? Are you investigating a murder?"

"No," Davis replied. "It's not murder. We don't know for sure a murder's been committed. We've simply found a human body by virtue of an anonymous note sent to Detective Fulford. We think your son might have written that note. I assure you, if he did write it, he did nothing wrong."

"Telling the police he made an unusual discovery is commendable," Fulford said. "We think if Donnie did find the body, he may have seen something at the time that could be of help to us."

Mrs. Grey seemed resigned. She nodded in agreement and called out, "Donnie, please come here. Some people want to talk to you."

She faced the detectives with a pleading expression. "You will be gentle with him, won't you?"

They nodded reassuringly as Donnie entered the room. He smiled at the two officers but fastened his eyes firmly on Leda Fulford.

"You're the pretty lady I met two days ago, aren't you?" he said. "I'm glad to see you."

"And I'm glad to see you," Fulford said. "I want you to be my friend."

Donnie seemed pleased. He grinned with pleasure. "I'll be your friend if you'll be mine. Will you?"

"Of course I will. Now that we're friends, I want you to do something for me. Will you look at this?"

She handed him the note. He took it, glanced briefly at it, and smiled in a conspiratorial way. He seemed pleased at the interest shown by the detectives.

"Did you write that, Donnie?" Fulford asked.

"It's a riddle," Donnie said. "I'll bet it took you a while to figure it out."

"Yes," Fulford said. "It did. It's very clever. Did it take you a long time to make it up?"

Donnie seemed to scoff at the question. "No, ma'am. You should see how fast I can do the Jumble and the Cryptoquote," he said proudly.

"I'll bet you're a regular whiz," Fulford said.

"I can do the Jumble faster than anyone," he said, a note of challenge in his voice.

"You could beat me, I'm sure," Davis said. "I'm pretty good at the Cryptoquote, but the Jumble stumps me at times." He gave Donnie a half-honest, half-feigned look of admiration and followed it with a coaxing inquiry. "Donnie, did you find a young woman's body while you were bird-watching near Proctor Creek?"

"I was watching a shrike, a butcher bird," Donnie said diffidently. "He caught a minnow and flew into the bushes with it. I watched him stick the little fish onto a thorn. Then he swooped down and caught one of those little green lizards. He stuck it on a thorn while it was still wiggling. That's the way they do it," he said. "They save what they catch to eat later."

"Donnie," Fulford said gently, "what about the body?"

"Well, that's when I saw it. While I was watching the butcher bird. She didn't have any clothes on. I looked at her a long time, but she never moved. Then I saw her arm had been cut off. That's when I knew something was wrong and I ought to tell somebody."

He looked directly at Fulford. "I remembered you from your visit to Sarah's place. I figured I would tell you. So I sent you the note."

"You did the right thing," Fulford assured him. "That's just what a good citizen is supposed to do."

Donnie responded to her praise. "At first I thought I'd make up a jumble. When you worked it, it would tell you to go to Proctor Creek. But I thought that was too easy. Detectives should have to find clues. It's not right to give them clues. So I hid the clue in a riddle. How long did it take you to figure it out?"

"A long time," Davis said. "It was a tough one."

"Donnie, did you see anything else when you found the body?" Fulford asked.

"I saw a couple of squirrels and a rabbit."

"What I mean, Donnie, is did you see any person or persons where you saw the body? Did you see any sign of someone having been there, like a boat tied up in the creek, a pickup truck, or a piece of clothing lying on the ground, or any footprints?"

Donnie's face assumed a sly expression. When he spoke, his voice lacked assurance. "There were lots of birds. I was busy watching them. I didn't see anything else."

Davis sensed his furtiveness. "Donnie, tell us the truth. It's very important. Did you see anyone or anything when you found the body?"

Donnie was annoyed. "I told you no," he said peevishly. He turned to his mother. "Mommy, can I go back to my room?"

"Yes, darling, you can," Mrs. Grey said with a defiant look at the officers.

Davis was angry. "I'm sorry you let him go, Mrs. Grey. We needed to press him a little harder. If Donnie saw someone place the body where he found it, and if that person was aware Donnie was watching, your son might be in danger. Do you understand what I'm saying?"

"I do, but I can't believe any such thing happened. If Donnie had seen anything odd when he found the body, he would have told you. He's as honest as the day is long."

Davis felt like arguing the point but said instead, "Will you please question him again, Mrs. Grey? If he tells you anything new, let us know."

"I will," she promised. "But I'm convinced he saw nothing."

"I hope you're right," Fulford said. "For Donnie's sake."

When they got back to division headquarters, they ran into Gerry Fillmore.

"I'm glad to see the two of you," he said, gesturing toward his office. "Come in here. I want to talk to you about the woman you found."

They sat, and Fillmore lit a cigar.

"Any idea who she is?"

"None," Davis said. "And little expectation of identifying her any time soon. Chris has examined her for signs that might point to her identity. So far nothing."

"We can always circulate a picture of her to the media."

"Or put her mug on milk cartons," Fulford said dryly.

"Don't knock traditional methods," Fillmore said. "They work. I admit they take a little time, but we have to find out who she is."

"I don't want to publish her picture immediately," Davis said. "Can you imagine the shock to her family? They think she's resting peacefully in her grave, and suddenly they see her picture and learn she's been dug up. I don't want to subject them to that unless it's absolutely necessary. I'd prefer to try identifying her some other way."

"All right," said Fillmore. "You got a point, but if we can't find out who she is in a few days, we'll have to publish her picture. How about the guy who dumped her in the creek?"

"She wasn't dumped in the creek," Fulford said. "Whoever did it just laid her out on the bank."

Fillmore disregarded the correction. "Decent of him, wasn't it? I assume you think it was a man?"

"Seems likely," said Davis. "I can't imagine a woman abducting the body of a female and hiding it in the woods."

"It's not a woman's thing, is it?" Fillmore said. "What about the man who found her?"

"His name is Donovan Grey," Davis said. "He's twenty-four years old and retarded, but he's not so dumb. He found her while bird-watching and sent Leda a note telling her where to find the body."

Fillmore knotted his forehead into a lattice of wrinkles and scratched his chin. "You don't suppose he put the body there himself and made up the story about finding her while bird-watching?"

"He could have," Fulford said. "It's certainly possible, but when we talked with him, we got the impression he was telling the truth. That he really discovered the body the way he said."

Fillmore seemed not to have heard her, his mind absorbed in its own train of thought. "One thing makes him an unlikely suspect. Where in the devil would a retarded man get his hands on the embalmed body of a young girl?"

"The question applies to more than Donnie," Davis said. "Where would anybody get hold of an embalmed body? That question has driven us up the wall. Logically, you have to assume an embalmed body could only have been stolen from a cemetery or a mortuary. But we've been assured by experts that such a theft is highly improbable. So, where do we turn next?"

Fillmore smiled one of his insufferably superior smiles, the kind he adopted when he was about to enjoy a bit of one-upmanship.

"There's another possibility," he said. "I'm surprised you haven't thought of it. She might have come from a medical school laboratory. They use cadavers to teach anatomy, don't they? Surgery, too, I suppose."

"We've thought of that," Davis said, a smug expression revealing his pleasure at being able to deflate Fillmore. "We ruled it out because the body showed no signs of being dissected. She's still pretty much in one piece."

"Her arm was cut off, wasn't it?" countered Fillmore. "If that isn't dissection, I don't know what is."

"You're stretching the term dissection a bit, aren't you?" Fulford asked.

"Students have to be taught amputation of limbs. So someone used her to demonstrate how to amputate an arm."

"It's a possibility," Davis admitted reluctantly. He knew Fillmore was giving him a directive, and it was useless to protest.

"We'll follow up on it."

"Southeastern Med. School would be a good place to start, I'd think," said Fillmore. He paused, thinking. "As for that kid, Donovan Grey, have you considered the possibility that he might have seen something when he found the body that could point you to the guy who dumped her?"

"We have. He got evasive when we asked him that question. We wanted to press him but couldn't. His mother wouldn't let us. When she saw we were upsetting him, she told him he could go to his room and not answer any more questions."

"Well, somehow you'd better get some straight answers from him."

"The question is, how do we do it? Want us to drag him into the station on suspicion, subject him to team interrogation?"

Fillmore snorted. "Don't be stupid. Be creative."

Chapter Four

Davis and Fulford sat looking at one another, unable to hide their sense of weariness.

"I can't remember a case," Davis said, "that has been more frustrating. We can't seem to get a handle on it. We had one hell of a time locating this woman's body, and now that we've found her, we can't tell who she is. How, I ask you, can we make an intelligent move?"

Fulford shook her head. "I'm a poor one to ask for advice. This is my first case, and it's not what I'd call an easy one. I guess Fillmore is right. The only thing we should do is make one more try at identifying her."

"We need a break, Leda, a new piece of evidence. Something that will add a new dimension to the puzzle."

As he stared gloomily at the floor, the telephone rang. Davis lifted the receiver and said, "Chris. Good to hear from you. What's up?"

"You'll never believe this, Wade," Chris said. "Not in a million years."

"Try me," Davis replied. "I can believe a dozen impossible things before breakfast."

"You may have trouble with this one. Your one-armed, adolescent corpse has been raped. That is, if a dead body can be raped. His tone of voice reflected his incredulity.

Davis was dumfounded. "She was what?"

"Raped, man. There's semen in her vagina and traces of what I think is a common lubricating jelly in her vulva."

"Someone had intercourse with her dead body? The idea turns my stomach." Davis's tone was unbelieving.

"Mine, too, but it happened. And it must have been done just a few hours before her body was found. I don't think semen would last very long under such circumstances."

"How did you find this out, Chris? Surely you didn't give her a vaginal exam?"

"Of course not. And I didn't bother to cut her open the way you suggested. I did examine her body for traces of mold, insect bites, or other signs that vermin might have been at her. Then I noticed seepage from the vagina. I knew what it was, but I put some on a slide and confirmed my guess."

Davis was having difficulty crediting Chris's revelation. It was too far outside his notion of what depraved human beings could do to be taken in swiftly. "Jesus, Chris, this is the weirdest thing I ever heard of."

"It's weird, all right. We're dealing with something called necrophilia, an abnormal attraction to dead bodies. When it occurs in men, it often involves intercourse with a corpse."

Davis found the idea revolting. "Isn't it practically impossible to have intercourse with a dead person?"

"No. It's just as simple as with a live person. A little lubrication to aid penetration is all it takes. In fact, sodomy would be quite feasible."

"Was she sodomized, too?"

"No. No, I was just saying that, although sodomy is more difficult, it could have been done."

Davis was silent. He had seen human behavior, brutal and gross beyond imagining, many times before: people burned to death with acid, murdered bodies with mutilated sex organs, victims with eyes gouged out, children impaled on fence pickets, men with guts spilling out from machete wounds. But this was a different kind of abomination, something he had never experienced before or thought of in his wildest imagining.

He hung up the phone and turned to look at Fulford. "I'm sure you gathered from my remarks what Chris told me, but let me elaborate a bit."

He watched the revulsion spread across her face as he spoke. She shook her head as if to dislodge a loathsome image from her mind.

"I've heard of necrophilia, Wade. But I never expected to be confronted with a case of it. It shakes you, doesn't it. For someone to defile the body of that sweet little girl is beyond imagining. Only a twisted, wicked, diabolical man could have done such a thing."

"Well," Wade said, "there are plenty of that kind around."

Several moments elapsed as they pondered their next move. Fulford got on the phone to Art Walker of Art's Crafts to reaffirm the identity of the professor who was a prolific leaded glass artist, exhibiting in area arts and crafts shows. His name, as Art had told her, was Ralph Hamlet, but he was not a member of the faculty at Emory University but was a professor at Southeastern U. Fulford noted that Bankhead Road originated less than a mile from the southwest corner of the Southeastern campus. They decided, however, to postpone an interview with Hamlet for the time being.

"We're dealing with a retarded man and a sexual deviate," Davis said. "I think we need to talk to an expert in abnormal psychology. Somebody who can give us a little grounding. I've been in touch with a Dr. Emma Zorn, a specialist in deviant behavior, and she's agreed to talk with us. We can be in her office within a few minutes if we start now."

"My calendar is clear," Fulford said. "Let's go."

Zorn reminded Davis of the Sunday school teacher under whose tutelage he had suffered as a boy. Hair done up in a bouffant style, wire-rimmed glasses perched on an eagle's beak nose, chin thrust forward belligerently, she presented a formidable aspect. However, she was soft-spoken, gentle of manner, and, while pedantic in speech, was refreshingly unpretentious.

"We are dealing in an area that is little understood," she said after Davis and Fulford had been seated and pleasantries had been exchanged. "Most of the information we have about sexual aberration comes from clinical cases described by psychiatrists or written up in crime literature. Most of the agreed-upon stuff is descriptive, not causative."

"Okay," said Davis, "let's begin with the descriptive stuff."

"The lore goes back to Krafft-Ebbing, a German psychiatrist," said Zorn. "He wrote a book, *Psychopathia Sexualis,* in eighteen eighty-six, in which he described a number of pathologies, among them pedophilia and homosexuality. The latter is no longer considered a pathology."

Davis wished she would get on with it. He and Fulford were interested solely in necrophilia and could live without an account of other sexual deviations. But it was not reasonable, he assumed, to suppose a pedagogue would forgo the chance to instruct an audience.

"Krafft-Ebbing devoted a lot of time to what we now call paraphilias," she went on. "Paraphilia means, roughly speaking, wrongheaded or harmful sexual behaviors. In addition to homosexuality, which was then considered abnormal, and pedophilia, he described exhibitionism, fetishism, masochism, voyeurism, and necrophilia."

"We're interested in necrophilia," Fulford said. "We know what kind of behavior it is, at least in general, but we were hoping you might be able to give us a profile of a person who exhibits such a, what did you call it, paraphilia?"

"I doubt I can help you much," Zorn said. "Necrophilia is extremely rare. I have never seen a necrophiliac—personally, I mean—nor have I read of more than a few cases. Some years ago, the papers devoted a lot of space to a man called Geen, who had robbed a dozen or more graves of females and kept the bodies in his basement. After his arrest, he admitted to having had intercourse with some, and having masturbated while fondling others.

"He mutilated one of the bodies by making an incision all the way around the chest, above and below the breasts, and stripping the skin away. He had, as a result, a kind of brassiere, which he wore while fondling the other bodies and masturbating."

Davis was repulsed at this description of Geen's behavior. "The man must have been insane. No normal person would do a thing like that."

"Well, Geen was locked up in an asylum, so, legally, he was insane. Such people are called psychopaths or sociopaths. They know their behavior is wrong, but they are unwilling or unable to restrain themselves. They often go to great lengths to conceal or camouflage their deviance."

"Can you give us specific indicators of a necrophiliac's personality?" Davis asked.

"I'll try. First of all, a necrophiliac is male. I suppose there have been cases of females with an unnatural attraction for the dead, but I've never heard of one, nor have I read of one in the literature. That may simply be because the kind of behavior they indulge in doesn't draw attention to itself. All the cases I know of have been male. He, the male necrophiliac, would be fairly young. After forty or fifty, the male sex drive diminishes. Although age might reduce sexual activity, reduced sexual drive is not responsible for the decline. The reason necrophiliacs are usually youthful is that by forty or fifty they are likely to have been apprehended.

"To his neighbors and acquaintances, he would appear normal, even friendly and likable. He would be good at dissembling, skillfully concealing his true attitudes and feelings. He would not think his behavior was wrong; hence, he would not feel guilt or shame. His emotions would be superficial. He would have no real affection for women, or for friends and relatives."

She paused, her facial expression and attitude skeptical. "This so-called profile is of dubious value. Most of the items are after-the-fact observations. How you would detect them in a potential psychopath is beyond me. And, you should note, normal people sometimes exhibit these same characteristics."

"We have a suspect," Davis said. "Let me describe him to you. Then you can tell me if you think he might have had intercourse with the body of a young female."

"I'll try," Zorn said, "but please remember, my opinion will not be very reliable."

"Understood," Davis said. "In our profession, we often have to rely heavily on the best opinion we can get." He paused, assembling his thoughts.

"We have a young man, twenty-four years of age, but mentally retarded. We are told he has the mental capacity of a ten-year-old. He is able to work. Holds a job in a colored glass studio and is independent enough to work out in a gym and do bird-watching on his own. He is fully developed sexually, and his mother is concerned about how he satisfies his erotic urges. We know she has encouraged him to masturbate, but when we first met him, he showed an interest in Detective Fulford which, while childlike in a way, seemed also to be erotic."

"Not surprising, if he's a masturbator," Zorn said. "A man almost always fantasizes he's having intercourse with a desirable female while he masturbates. I'd say that's probably why this young man was so taken by Ms. Fulford. She would undoubtedly enhance his next episode of erotic stimulation."

"I'm flattered," Fulford said dryly.

"In this business," Zorn said, "we tell things like they are. The notion may be distasteful to you, Ms. Fulford, but it's probably true."

She drummed lightly with her fingers on the desk top and spoke thoughtfully, "You asked if the subject you've described could have had intercourse with the corpse of a young woman, and I must tell you it is my opinion he did not. I base my judgment on several factors. First, his mother has taught him to express his sexual urges in a socially acceptable way. Second, he has undoubtedly been admonished to leave women alone. He would know that having intercourse with a woman, particularly a dead woman, is wrong. Also, you tell me he does not exhibit deceit; in fact, you tell me he is refreshingly candid. Though you have not explicitly said so, I infer he shows genuine regard for his mother and his coworkers in the glass shop. These are not the traits of a sociopath."

Davis and Fulford received her opinion with relief. Neither had much stomach for arresting Donovan Grey and explaining to his mother their reason for doing so.

They returned from their interview with Zorn and planned their next move. Earlier, they had decided their best prospect of tracing a perpetrator would be through investigating persons who had access to came. The man who, according to the records of crafts shops, used came in the greatest quantities was Ralph Hamlet of Southeastern University. Fillmore, however, had let them know he thought they should first continue the search for the identity of the young woman's body.

"So," Davis said to his companion, "shall we tackle Ralph Hamlet, as we had planned, or shall we try Severson of Southeastern Med. first?"

"I'll vote for Severson," Fulford said. "We still don't know where the girl's body came from. If Severson tells us she couldn't have been one of his cadavers, I'd like to know that. We'll really be up the creek."

"If you meant that as a joke," Davis said, "you ought to be sent to your room."

Fulford cringed with pretended guilt. "Honestly, all I meant was if she didn't come from a graveyard, a mortuary, or a medical school lab, where did she come from? There aren't any other possibilities."

"I can think of one. It's pretty far-fetched, but it's a possibility. Let's assume she was murdered by our necrophiliac to feed his lust for the nonliving body. He wants to keep her fresh and available for a long time. So he learns the art of embalming. Takes a lesson or two, let's suppose, from the Cawthon School of Burial Science. Embalming is not all that complicated. After he's picked up the rudiments, he begins to assemble a harem of female bodies."

"Very ingenious, Wade," Fulford said, "and given the fact that a necrophiliac is a certified psychopath, it has a lot of plausibility. Only thing I can't see, however, is why he cut off her arm and tossed it into the Chattahoochee."

"Yeah," Davis said. "It doesn't make much sense, even for a sociopath."

They sat pondering the unsavory action for which they could find no sane explanation. Davis reminded himself that, according to the experts, perversion has its own logic. Find the premise for it, and the act will make sense. Unfortunately, he could find no acceptable premise.

They left the office, climbed into a red-and-white, and in twenty minutes were at Southeastern University.

A secretary ushered them into the office of Pemberton Severson, professor of anatomy and chairman of the Department of Biological Science at Southeastern University. The office was big enough, in Davis's opinion, for two ordinary offices, but he quickly perceived that Severson was a man of no ordinary stature. The office furnishings were ornate and expensive, with one wall devoted entirely to Severson's degrees, graduate diplomas, memberships in professional organizations, and commendations from humanitarian associations. In blank spaces among these credentials were signed photographs of some of Atlanta's movers and shakers. Davis felt he should have been overwhelmed but for some reason was not.

Severson was obliging but condescending. He treated the detectives as if they were ignoramuses to be tolerated out of a sense of civic duty.

"I would have thought," he said in response to Davis's question, "the police would have had prior experience with the use of cadavers in medical schools."

Davis kept his irritation in check. "We know that medical schools use human bodies for instructional purposes," he said quietly, "but we don't know how such bodies are acquired, where and how you keep them, or what you do with them when they have served their purposes. If you could help us on those points, we would appreciate it."

"As to the first question," Severson said, "there are several answers. Some people will their bodies to us. We buy a few bodies by paying their owners cash prior to their death. But most of the bodies we get from city and county authorities who must dispose of homeless vagrants whose bodies are unclaimed."

He looked at the detectives with a trace of covert disdain, assuming the expression of resignation a parent might use in humoring an overly curious child. "As for question number two, if you will come this way, I will show you how we keep our specimens."

He ushered them into a large room containing a dozen tables, each approximately eight by three feet wide, standing about waist high. Topped with what looked like gray slate slabs, they all had a rim about two inches high around the edge and a drain at one end.

"During instruction," he said, "specimens are laid out on these tables for examination and dissection. When class ends, the bodies are preserved in tanks of a solution called Biostat, nothing more than a formaldehyde mixture." He pointed to a row of tanks with synthetic tarpaulins stretched over them.

"Two students are assigned to each specimen," he continued, "and they work on the same body the entire semester. As the body is dissected, the parts are placed in a cloth bag and kept in the tank with the rest of the body. At the end of the semester, the body and all separate parts are cremated, and the ashes are given to relatives or are buried as circumstances indicate."

"I suppose you know the identity of each cadaver," Fulford said, "and would know if one of them disappeared."

"Are you thinking we might have a problem with security? That someone might make off with a body, or perhaps a part of it? I sense from your questions that you may be on the trail of a body snatcher."

"You've guessed the purpose of our visit," Davis admitted. "I suppose we should have told you of it earlier. We are trying to find out where a woman's body, embalmed and abandoned in a rural area, came from."

"May I ask what shape the body was in when you found it?"

"Relatively fresh, according to our medical examiner, and intact, except one arm was missing."

Severson said, "Ah!" The sound seemed to reflect a strong sense of conviction. "Nothing else? Just the arm?"

"That's it."

"Did she have a full head of hair?"

"What significance could that have?" Fulford asked.

"When we receive a body," Severson said, "we shave all its hair, everything, before it's immersed in a preservative bath. Moreover, dissection begins with the removal of the skin from the back. We'd never remove an arm first. So you see, your corpse could not have been one of ours."

"Yeah," Davis said. "That seems evident, but she had to come from somewhere."

"I assume you've considered grave robbery."

"Yes, but we've been told robbing graves these days is almost impossible."

"Don't believe it. You may have been told that security in a particular cemetery is so effective, no one could have robbed one of its graves. No security system is foolproof. My guess is your body was dug up from a grave, and the cemetery people just haven't discovered the theft."

Davis was impressed with Severson's statement. The body had to come from somewhere, and in spite of assurances to the contrary, a graveyard seemed to be the best bet.

"I'm inclined to agree with you," he said, then added, "Thanks for your time."

They left Severson, who, though still smiling in a superior way, now seemed to have acquired a modicum of respect for the law.

The drive back to the office was a time of sober reflection. The introspective mood that fell over them was heightened by the dark sky and the curtains of rain that fell from clouds that seemed to hover just a few score feet above the ground.

Above the hum of the windshield wipers, distant thunder rumbled.

"Not a day to inspire optimism," Fulford said.

"No more than Severson did," Davis replied. "I think we've gone as far up this road as we ought to go. Let's waste no more time trying to find out where she came from. I doubt it would help us if we did know. When we find the person who mutilated her, we'll find out where he got her."

Back at headquarters, they bought coffee from the machine, retired to Davis's office, and took stock.

"Let's go back to people who had access to came," Fulford said. "Donnie Grey certainly did, but his telling us the location of the body was not the act of a guilty person. And Dr. Zorn didn't think him capable of the act.

"So . . . could any other employee of Bernhardt's Glass have some connection with the crime? No. For the simple reason they're all women and this is a man's crime."

Davis, who had been listening to her attentively, nodded his head in agreement. "Let's look at the ones we know about. There's Art himself. Right now we have no reason to believe he's involved. I only mention his name because he had access to came. There's nothing else to suggest he had anything to do with the crime."

"And that will be true of all the others," Fulford said. "The mere possession of came means, by itself, nothing. But it suggests a possible connection, a connection we'll have to follow up on and hope for a break."

"Art has steered us to Ralph Hamlet," Davis said, "but we haven't contacted Melissa's Arts and Crafts, Everyman's Hobby, and Atlanta Stained Glass. Maybe we can do this by telephone. Let's try."

Fulford phoned Melissa of Melissa's Arts and Crafts.

"I have only two customers who work in colored glass," she told Fulford. "One of them is a retired M.D. who lives in Buckhead. I just love him. He's the sweetest person you'd ever want to meet. Has a wonderful sense of humor. It's a good thing, too. His wife died just a few months ago, and I know he's terribly lonely. I think he took up glassmaking as a way a diverting his mind from the loss of his wife."

Not a very likely candidate for our perpetrator, Fulford thought. "Who's the other one," she asked Melissa.

"His name is Jakes. He always pays in cash, but I make out the receipt to Jakes. Someone told me he's an undertaker, and, out of curiosity, I looked him up in the yellow pages. He has an establishment in Rockdale, not far from the river. I'd say he's about thirty-five. He doesn't talk much but seems friendly enough."

Fulford thought Jakes was a man worthy of further attention. "He's an undertaker," she told Davis. "An undertaker sure has the opportunity to get his hands on a body."

"Indeed he does," Davis replied. "And I'll tell you someone else who'd have no trouble making off with a body: Baxter Cawthon, of Cawthon's School of Burial Science.

"I'm a bit encouraged by this line of investigation," he said, as he scanned the list of persons yet to be contacted. "I'm going to skip Atlanta Stained Glass. It's run by three women, and they do not sell came, but I'll have a go with Everyman's Hobby."

"Elmer Schultz," a voice said in response to Davis's call. "How can Everyman's Hobby help you?"

"I'm Detective Davis of the Atlanta Police Department. We're investigating a case that involves a person known to have done stained glass work—"

Schultz's voice interrupted, "Did you know, Inspector, that the art of constructing windows of stained glass is one of the oldest art forms in the world?"

"No, I didn't," said Davis, ignoring the error in his rank. "What we want to find out, Mr. Schultz, is do you have any customers who buy came regularly?"

"I can't believe you didn't know that," said Schultz. "It has a glorious history. And it's a rewarding hobby. I make leaded glass panels myself. Some very artistic things, if I do say so myself. I wish you could see some of them. Why don't you come by the store someday? I'll give you a proper show."

"Thank you," said Davis, "I appreciate the invitation. But right at this moment, I need to know if you have any customers who buy came from you frequently."

"I can think of only one, a young man in his late twenties," Schultz finally said, "who buys several strips about every other week. I can't remember his name offhand, but I could get it from the file if you want. He never says much. I think I've heard him utter four or five connected sentences on only one occasion.

"I had said something about an upcoming meeting in Atlanta of the National Organization for Women. That caused him to really let go. He said NOW and the women's liberation movement consisted of a bunch of man-haters and radicals who do not represent women in general."

"Would you look in your file for his name and address?"

"Yes. It's Percy Guildford. He lives at 1020 Perimeter, near the Fulton County Airport."

Davis thanked him, put down the phone, and he and Fulford pooled their information.

"Now what?" Fulford asked. "We can't just say to these people, 'Because you're a purchaser of came, you're under suspicion of raping a dead body, and we'd like to ask you some nasty questions.' We'd be thrown out."

"We'll not talk to them personally—just contact friends, coworkers, acquaintances. We'll say the person is being considered for a position on the force. Hamlet, for example, as a part-time lecturer at the Police Academy, Jakes for a position with the M.E., anything that sounds plausible. We're just doing a routine background check."

"What about Percy Guildford? He's a totally unknown quantity."

Davis laughed. "How about a job in public relations? He sounds like just the type."

Chapter Five

At 6 P.M., Matilda Grey called Bernhardt's Glass and, in a voice quavering with anxiety, asked Sarah if Donovan was still at work.

"He left at three o'clock," Sarah told her. "He said he was going to meet you at the dentist. Didn't he show up?"

"We didn't have a dental appointment. I can't understand why he would tell you such a story. I'm worried to death about him."

Sarah was puzzled as well as worried. It was unlike Donovan to tell a lie. He was too guileless, too open. Nevertheless, he had, when he left early, given her an excuse that was patently false. Something extraordinary must have induced him to do so.

"I don't know what to tell you, Mrs. Grey. Have you checked the gym? Perhaps he left early to get a good workout." She thought that eventuality was unlikely, but she was grasping at straws.

"I called the gym. He's not there. I don't know what to think. He's never done anything like this before. Should I call the police?"

"The police don't consider a person missing who has been gone just a few hours. I think it would be a waste of time to call 911. They'd just tell you to wait a while and call back again if he doesn't turn up. Why don't you call that detective, Wade Davis. He knows all about Donnie's finding that body. I'm sure he would be concerned."

"Of course I'm concerned," Davis told Mrs. Grey. "I very much fear Donnie saw something the day he discovered that young woman's body, something that made him a menace to her abductor. His life could be in danger."

"Please," Mrs. Grey implored, a strangled sob in her voice, "will you have some of your people look for him?"

Davis, fearing that Donovan might already be dead, assured her he would initiate a search at once. "We'll begin looking at Proctor

Creek. I think he may have gone there."

He hung up the phone and said to Fulford, "Donovan Grey has disappeared. He left work at three and hasn't been seen since. My guess is he's gone to Proctor Creek, where, I fear, someone is waiting who plans to do him harm. Probably already has."

"Donnie wouldn't go to meet just anyone at Proctor Creek," Fulford protested. "As simple-minded as he is, he would sense danger if a stranger asked him to come there."

"I don't think anyone asked him to come there," Davis replied. "I think he was lured to Proctor Creek by a ruse of some sort. He's an enthusiastic bird-watcher. If he were told that some rare bird, one that is practically unknown in these parts, had been sighted at Proctor Creek, he'd head there in a flash."

"Then we'd better get out there, too, hadn't we?"

Accompanied by a van carrying ten officers, Davis and Fulford drove to the mouth of Proctor Creek. Davis figured five people, walking abreast and a couple of yards apart on either side of the stream, could sweep an area wide enough to locate Donovan if he were anywhere near the stream. Davis prayed Donovan would be found, unharmed, hiding in a clump of bushes, perhaps, focusing on some rare bird. He told himself, however, that such a happy outcome was more wishful thinking than likelihood.

Davis assembled the searchers for final instructions. He spoke to them in a somber voice, "You will be looking for a young man who is intellectually challenged. He has the mental ability of a ten-year-old, but he is good-natured and likable. He can be easily frightened. In fact, your mere presence may alarm him. He's like a child. If you find him, assure him you are friends. Tell him his mother asked you to find him."

He paused, wondering what else to say.

"I'm assuming you will find him alive. I sincerely hope you will. If alive, he may have been beaten, possibly severely. I must also warn you that he may have been murdered. So be alert for the discovery of a body."

In the fading light, with ominous expectations, the searchers began. Walking a few feet apart, they scanned the underbrush, using flashlights because of the growing darkness, forcing their way through dense thickets, peering into every spot that might provide concealment for a secretive youth—or for his body. With the undergrowth clinging tenaciously to feet and legs, the going was slow.

After half a mile, a powerful flashlight beam from the hand of one of the crew on the north side of the creek fell upon the figure of a man, standing perhaps twenty feet away, but bent over, as if stooping to pick up something from the ground. The figure seemed to be peering downward into a stand of bamboo, whose thick, sturdy stems created a dense mass of foliage.

"Here, son," an officer called. "We're friends of your mom. She asked us to look for you. We've come to take you home."

The figure did not respond. It stood there immobile, bent over in that odd way, seeming, almost, about to topple to the ground.

Davis and Fulford, having been summoned to the scene, walked slowly toward the figure.

"Donnie," Davis called out. "It's Detectives Davis and Fulford."

Silence. Unnatural, puzzling silence.

When they pressed forward, the reason for Donovan's silence became apparent. He was dead—impaled upon a shaft of bamboo. Cut off about four feet from the ground and sharpened, the bamboo stem pierced his body just below the sternum. Almost two inches in diameter, it was strong enough to support him in that strange semi-crouched position.

The officers who had participated in the search stared in morbid fascination. Davis motioned for them to move back.

"Let's not disturb anything," he cautioned. "And don't trample the ground around him. You can look, but don't touch anything until the forensics people get here."

A distant peal of thunder shook the air. "I hope they come soon," Davis said aloud to no one in particular. "The rain will make a mess of every shred of evidence."

When Davis looked more closely at the body, he saw blood caked around a depression in the back of Donovan's head.

"I think," he said to Fulford, "he was struck a lethal blow before he was thrust upon the stake. I hope so. I hope he was spared the agony of that last brutal act."

Fulford had tears in her eyes.

"I can't forgive myself," she said. "We knew he saw something the day he found the body. We knew he was in grave danger. Why didn't we keep a closer eye on him?"

"We didn't know for sure he had seen anything. We couldn't follow him around on the basis of a hunch. His mother wouldn't let us worm the truth out of him. I wonder how she'll feel now."

"She'll be devastated. Her sweet and simple boy is dead because she wanted to protect him from intrusive police officers."

The crime scene officers were the first to arrive. Their flashlights blinked in the dark like giant fireflies as they raked through the dirt around Donovan's body and flailed the underbrush, seeking unlikely clues. With yellow tape, they framed the scene as if it were a surrealistic painting or a museum diorama.

Christopher McCalmon was out of sorts when he arrived.

"Jesus, Wade, I was just sitting down to curried lamb."

He saw Fulford and made an impudent face at her. Her contemptuous look sobered him.

"Sorry. Can't help being irreverent."

Seeing Donovan's outlandish posture, he became subdued and behaved with official detachment. He examined the wound where the stake entered Donovan's body. He probed with a gloved finger the depth and direction of the penetration. Then he examined the skull, palpating the bone around the fracture.

"He was dead, you know, when he was stuck on this thing. I'm surprised he stayed erect. If he hadn't been so well balanced, he would have rolled sidewise and hung like a worm on a hook."

"Masterful figure of speech," Davis said. "Any idea how long he's been dead?"

"Three, four hours at most, maybe less. His temperature is almost normal."

"And the weapon used on his skull?"

"A rock, maybe, a club of some kind, a wrench. It made a ragged depression about three quarters of an inch deep. I would guess it killed him instantly."

"We've found no sign of a weapon," Davis said. "Nor much of anything, really. Our murderer was a careful guy. The things we've found belong to the victim. A small backpack, a pair of binoculars, a notebook. His cap. I doubt if forensics will find anything useful in the lot."

"And I doubt if the postmortem will give you much help," Chris volunteered. "I'll do it the first thing in the morning. You're invited."

"Thanks," Davis said. "I'll take a rain check. Wouldn't want to get in your way."

It had begun to rain, not hard yet, but it was building up, Davis believed, toward one of the region's famous frog stranglers. "These forensic guys better hurry up," he said to Fulford. "The rain will soon obliterate any clues there might have been."

He turned to the officer who was putting Donovan's things in a large paper bag.

"Can I look at the last page of that notebook? I mean the last page the victim wrote on."

"If you're careful," the man said. He was sheltering the book under his jacket to protect it from the rain. He wore thin plastic gloves and cautiously lifted the leaves until he came to the last page bearing Donovan's writing. "Not much here," he observed as he handed the book over to Davis, who carefully guarded it from the rain.

But Davis and Fulford found the few words, presumably written in Donovan's hand, enlightening.

Ivory-billed Woodpecker
Proctor Creek
Pileated?

Davis looked at his companion. "What do you make of that, Leda?"

"Someone told Donnie an ivory-billed woodpecker had been sighted near Proctor Creek and probably urged him to have a look. Donnie went, probably very excited. But he feared the ivory-billed bird might have been confused with the pileated."

"I seem to remember that ivory-billed woodpeckers are practically extinct," Davis said, "but now and then supposed sightings have been reported. Donnie was such a bird enthusiast, he would have been eager to confirm an alleged sighting. But he was shrewd enough to know the sighting might have been an error. Too bad he didn't respect the odds and refuse to be tempted."

The rain fell in torrents. As they ran for their car, the hard ground beneath their feet began turning to muck.

Donovan's death confirmed their belief that further attempts to discover where the embalmed body had come from would be fruitless.

"Let's do as we had decided earlier," Davis said, "and look into the background of the people we know had access to came. One of the persons on that list was seen, I feel, by Donovan as he hid the body. And Donovan, unfortunately, was seen by him. Perceiving him to be a potential threat, that person lured him to the creek, smashed him over the head, and in a brutal act of vengeance, impaled him on a stalk of bamboo."

"We've agreed this is a man's crime, haven't we?" Fulford said. "That excludes from our list of came users Marygold McAllister, Sarah Bernhardt and the rest of her female crew, and the three women who own and operate Atlanta Stained Glass."

"The men remain on our active list," Davis said. "One of them may well have been Donovan's murderer."

"So, let's review the list," Fulford said, "and decide how we'll tackle the people on it. Here's the names of the men as I remember. There's Art Walker, of Art's Crafts, and Ralph Hamlet, one of Art's customers and a professor at Southeastern. Then there's Philip Baird, a customer of Melissa's Arts and Crafts and a retired M.D. living in Buckhead, and Garner Jakes, an undertaker, also a customer of Melissa's. Finally, Elmer Schultz, proprietor of Everyman's Hobby, and one of his customers, Percy Guildford."

She paused, thinking. "Have I left out anyone?"

"Not a soul. You've got a phenomenal memory, Leda. I doubt I could have reeled off those names so swiftly."

He had jotted the names down as she spoke and now laid the list between them for consideration. "Let's go over these names and try to apply Zorn's profile of a necrophiliac. I know she thinks her list is of doubtful value, but it's a place to start."

"It will help us eliminate some of the names," Fulford said. "For instance, there's that retired M.D., Philip Baird. According to Melissa, he's in his sixties, at least. That puts him beyond the time when sexual need would drive him to find relief in a dead body."

"Agreed. I'm crossing him off the list. I'm inclined to do the same with Art Walker. I don't think he's quite as old as Baird, but not far off. Old enough, I think, to be an unlikely candidate.

"Art gave us a good prospect, however, in Ralph Hamlet, the professor at Southeastern. He's young, unmarried, and has access to a lot of came. Those things don't mean much by themselves, but they suggest further investigation might prove fruitful."

"My most likely candidate," said Fulford, "is Garner Jakes. Melissa told us he makes himself likable, falls into the right age category, and, most suggestive, he's an undertaker. He'd have no trouble at all getting his hands on a dead body."

"I doubt it would be as easy as you think, even for an undertaker, but I agree he's a good bet. Elmer Schultz mentioned a man we shouldn't dismiss, Percy Guildford. He's young, introverted, and seems to be a woman-hater. Especially dislikes radical feminists."

"What about Schultz himself? He's in the age range. Doesn't fit anything else in the profile, though. But he works in stained glass and thinks it's an ancient and honorable art form. That's not very much, is it?"

"For the time being, I'm willing to put him on hold."

Davis sat back, put his feet on a pulled-out lower desk drawer, and stared at his colleague. She was studying the list attentively. They had worked together a little over two weeks now. Not enough time for him to form a reliable judgment, but he believed Fulford to be one of those rare persons whose intrinsic worth, like precious metal, is at once evident.

He would trust her to investigate Garner Jakes, the undertaker.

The phone rang imperiously, but Davis's concentration was so intense, he barely heard it. He was sketching in his mind a probable modus operandi for the killer who had done away with Donovan Grey. The perpetrator must have suddenly been faced with a compelling reason for disposing of the body of the young woman he had just violated. Davis could not imagine what that reason could have been, but whatever it was, it had required swift action.

For some reason he took the body to Proctor Creek, probably in a car or a pickup truck. Davis believed he either intended to hide the body to be retrieved later, or he intended to dispose of her completely. It was reasonable to assume a necrophiliac would have a streak of sadism in him toward women. Perhaps he planned to cut up the body and throw the pieces into the stream. Donovan must have come upon him as he was cutting off the arm to throw into the creek. Donovan, sensing danger, fled, but not before the culprit saw him.

Davis felt sure, after carefully reviewing his thoughts, that he had constructed a probable explanation of the events leading to Donovan's murder.

He was so engrossed in his task, he forgot about the post-mortem on Donovan's body, and he suddenly became aware of the insistent ringing of the phone. When he lifted the receiver, Chris's peevish voice assailed his ear.

"Hell, Wade. Don't you ever answer the phone? Get an answering machine so people don't waste their time trying to rouse you."

"Sorry, I was busy. I've got an answering machine, but like a lot of things around here, it's not working."

"What were you so busy doing you couldn't hear the phone? Playing with your sexy colleague?"

The remark annoyed Davis. "Chris, did you call me just to be obnoxious, or have you got something to tell me?"

Chris's voice sounded incredulous as he said, "Donovan Grey was sodomized." He paused to let Davis digest the information. "Also, in case you're interested, he was dead by four o'clock at the latest. Since he left Bernhardt's Glass at three, he must have been murdered almost as soon as he got to Proctor Creek."

Davis said lamely, "Why am I so surprised? I knew we were dealing with a scumbag. I assume Grey was dead when the rape occurred."

"There's no way to know for sure. But I'd guess a necrophiliac would be more likely to get a sexual charge out of a dead body, male or female, than a live one."

Davis called Fulford's number. She wasn't there. She was, he supposed, out trying to get a line on Garner Jakes. Knowing she would be appalled and disgusted, he was not eager to be the bearer of Chris's discoveries. He filed the news of the sexual assault on Grey in the back of his mind and decided to see what information he could unearth on Ralph Hamlet, the man who, Art Walker had said, was a prolific producer of stained glass artifacts.

The woman who answered the door was not at all what Davis expected. Rather than a matronly housewife, as would befit a street of middle-class family residences, she was—he could think of no other word to describe her—exotic. Her face was a mix of Asian and European features. Eyes slanted, forehead wide and high, nose and cheeks prominent, an Englishwoman's jaw. The garment she had wrapped around her was, he supposed, a sari.

"Sorry to bother you," he said, "but a neighbor of yours, I believe he lives just four doors down, has applied for a sensitive government position. His name's Ralph Hamlet, and we're obliged to do a background check on him."

She seemed pleased. "Professor Hamlet, of course. Won't you come in? My name's Simba."

It was not an ordinary dwelling Davis stepped into. It seemed a monument to disorder. A half dozen desks were scattered throughout the room without any distinguishable pattern. All were cluttered with books and magazines. The books, Davis saw, were mostly textbooks. A single computer, its screen dark, perched on a stand beside one of the desks.

Simba, following Davis's poorly disguised look of disapproval, smiled. "We're a kind of student co-op here. Six of us share the rent and other expenses. It's disorderly and crowded, but it's cheap, and we're near the campus. Everyone else is in class now, except me. I've got a bad case of PMS."

"I'm sorry to hear that," Davis said. "You're not too bad off to answer a few questions, are you?"

"No. I'm really just babying myself. Won't you sit down?"

Davis sat at one of the desks facing Simba. He found her attractive. She had draped herself, in a frankly sensuous way, on the only couch the room afforded, and her glance appeared to be inviting.

"Do you know Professor Hamlet personally?" he asked.

"Depends on what you mean by personally. At the beginning of the semester, several neighbors complained about this house being occupied by six unrelated people. The neighborhood, they said, was zoned for single-family dwellings, and we were turning it into a multiple-family place. They asked the city commission to evict us. Professor Hamlet was not one of the complainants, and because we were students, we thought he might help us. He agreed to do so and helped draw up an agreement between us and our neighbors. We promised to live quietly, to avoid partying and late-night comings and goings, things like that. The commission, with the consent of the neighbors, allowed us to stay as long as we kept to the agreement and behaved."

"So you sort of negotiated with him to gain his support."

"Exactly."

"And what was he like?"

"I thought he was a cold fish. I was ready to show my appreciation in a tangible way, but he wasn't having any."

"Did he try to date you? Anything like that? I assume there are other women in the house."

"Nothing but women. That was another condition of our being allowed to stay. No, he showed little interest in any of us. Some of us thought he might be gay."

"Did you ever talk to any of the neighbors about him?"

"No. The neighbors are not exactly in love with us, or with him."

"Did you ever take one of his courses?"

"No, but Kim did. If you want to talk to her, she'll be here any minute. I'd be glad to make you a cup of coffee while you're waiting."

"That would be nice. I'd appreciate it."

Simba retreated to the kitchen, but before she returned with the coffee, a thin young woman came up the steps and entered the room. Davis startled her as he rose to his feet and said, "You must be Kim."

"I am. You a friend of Simba's?"

"My name is Davis. I'm a policeman. I'm investigating one of your neighbors, Ralph Hamlet."

"Oh. Him. What's he done?"

"Nothing. He's being considered for a sensitive position, and we're running a routine background check on him. Simba told me you once took a course from him. What kind of impression did he make on you?"

She wrinkled her nose in an expression of distaste. "Well, he put the make on me, in case you're interested. Asked me to come to his house to see his stained glass work."

"Did you go?"

"Yeah. I was flattered. He's a big name in his field, you know. He's quite an artist, too. I was really impressed by the things he showed me."

"Does he have a workshop? Is that where he took you?"

"That's where he wanted to take me, but I wouldn't go. His so-called workshop is in an old bomb shelter in his back yard. He says it was built in the sixties when people were sure an atomic war was about to happen. Now it has no practical use, so he turned it into a studio. I'd seen the things he had in his house and was impressed by them, but I didn't care to see anymore. Nothing specific, you understand, but he was sending out signals every girl knows how to read. I figured if I didn't get out of there, he'd be after me to spend the night. I asked him to take me home."

"And did he?"

"Yes, he did. I give him that. He was perfectly sweet about it."

Davis searched for some sign in the face of the girl before him that would indicate she was not telling the truth or that she was stretching the truth to impress him. He found none. She seemed perfectly straightforward.

"What was the course you took from him?"

"It was called 'Art and Archeology of the Ancient Middle East.' It satisfied one of the general studies requirements or I never would have taken it. It covered Mesopotamia, Egypt, and the Holy Land."

Davis gave some thought to framing the next question. He wasn't quite sure how to word his inquiry. "I suppose you studied the customs of Middle Eastern countries, including such things as how they disposed of their dead?"

"That and marriage customs, business practices, banking and currency, and art and literature. Were you particularly interested in burial practices?"

"Not really," Davis said. "I just used it as an example."

"Well, you picked a good one. Professor Hamlet seemed especially interested in mummification and other means of preserving the dead. He spent several lectures describing how the Egyptians mummified bodies, omitting none of the gruesome details like evisceration and trepanning to empty the skull. It was yucky. Then he contrasted the Egyptian methods with modern embalming."

"How detailed was his discussion of modern embalming procedures?"

"He sounded like a mortician, as if he actually had experience in the business."

To Davis, this information suggested several fascinating avenues of speculation. He asked Kim for any additional information she might like to share, and, after she volunteered a few innocuous comments, he thanked her and Simba, who had been quietly sipping coffee during his interrogation of Kim, and left.

He called next on several neighbors, most of whom had little contact with Hamlet. His defense of the students, and the respondents' attitudes toward that defense, composed most of their testimony. Davis found one thing common to the remarks of Hamlet's neighbors, however. They found him to be aloof, distant. "A withdrawn, self-contained introvert," one man declared. Another called him "a surly, uncivil loner."

Davis concluded his investigation of Hamlet with a visit to the chairman of the Anthropology Department, Delbert Linn. Linn, a tall, slender, ascetic, scholarly type, was not at all amiable. His manner was courteous enough, he even invited Davis to have a cup of coffee, but his speech was acidic, almost vitriolic.

"I know you are simply discharging your duty, Detective Davis, but I must tell you I deplore the extent to which government is inclined to pry into the private lives of its citizens. You are the second FBI agent I have had to deal with this semester. It's becoming epidemic."

"I assure you, Mr. Linn, I am not an FBI agent," Davis said. "I am with the Atlanta Police, and there is nothing sinister about this inquiry. When your university hired Professor Hamlet, they investigated him thoroughly, I'm sure. We are thinking of possibly hiring Hamlet on an adjunct basis; hence, this inquiry."

"Well," Linn said grudgingly, "what would you like to know?"

"What is your general assessment of him?"

"Ralph Hamlet is a man of the highest integrity, a product of one of the best universities in the country, and a good teacher. He has acquired something of a reputation as an artist in leaded glass, but in spite of the time spent on this pursuit, he is still a formidable researcher."

"Is he married?"

"Not now. He was until his wife died about a year ago. Since then, he had shown little interest in the opposite sex."

"He's not gay, is he?"

"That's the kind of question, Detective Davis, I deplore," Linn said sternly. "What possible relevance could such a private matter have to you?"

"Given the climate of opinion in some quarters of government, it may have importance. However, you needn't answer if you choose not to."

"Unfortunately, if I don't answer, you'll conclude that he is. Let me just say this: Hamlet is circumspect and proper in his private affairs, as all of us should be." He gave Davis a hard look.

"Would you call him gregarious?"

"He rarely socializes with other members of the faculty. Oh, he attends parties at Thanksgiving and Christmas and goes to social functions as required by the university, but I wouldn't call him a social animal.

"Now, Detective Davis, if you've nothing else, I should get back to my work."

"Of course. And many thanks for your cooperation."

Fulford found the funeral home of Garner Jakes in Kenwood with little difficulty. Although it was situated at the edge of what appeared to be a well-to-do neighborhood, it was not an imposing establishment. It was a storefront.

When she talked with Jakes, pretending to be a customer interested in a prepaid funeral arrangement, she discovered the reason for his modest premises. He had been in business a mere eighteen months. The small inventory of caskets in his showroom suggested business was not booming. The thought of an undertaker unable to prosper for want of corpses amused her.

Jakes struck her as the commonest of common men. Physically, he was ordinary in every respect. His height, weight, facial structure, and body type would fall, she surmised, in the precise middle of a bell curve. Probably his temperament and intelligence, too. Such pop psychology, she reminded herself, was about as reliable as long-range weather forecasting. Nevertheless, she was convinced Jakes was not what he appeared to be, that he wore a facade of normality. A facade to conceal what? Probably incompetence and insecurity. She could not find a reason in his behavior to justify her estimate of him, but she supposed the impression came from subliminal cues, cues that affected her, but ones she was not consciously aware of.

Inquiries in the neighborhood provided Fulford with little that was noteworthy about Jakes. He had been in business a little over a year. He appeared to have few clients, was unmarried, was not friendly, but was cordial to customers and visitors. He drove a modest compact car and lived in a small, unpretentious house about three blocks away from his business.

"That's enough prying," Fulford said to herself. She had not expected to find any crucial information and had found nothing remarkable.

Davis had not actually told her to do so, but he had said, in a way that suggested he would be happy to be relieved of the responsibility, that someone needed to look into Percy Guildford's background. She thought she would show a little initiative and undertake the task.

Perimeter Street was in an area that had obviously been zoned for mixed structures. Apartment houses and condominiums were interspersed with duplexes and a few single-family dwellings. Guildford's address, ten-twenty, was a duplex. Fulford thought the people living in the attached dwelling next to him ought to know something about his habits and might even know him personally.

She rang the bell.

The man who answered the door gave her a start. She almost lost her composure. He was a policeman, tall, beefy, dressed in uniform, wearing a gun belt that held a Colt .45 semiautomatic pistol. He seemed as startled to see her as she was to see him. She fumbled for something to say.

He spoke first, "What the devil?" Then he laughed. "I suppose you're here to arrest me."

"Yeah," Fulford said with mock seriousness. "I've got a sheet on you a yard long."

"Well, come in. Don't stand out there in the cold. I'm about to leave for work, but you can meet the wife, and then maybe you'll tell me what this is all about."

Fulford entered a small, neat living room.

"I'm Benjamin Walpole, from Traffic Division," the policeman said. "And this is my wife, Jenny."

"Fulford. Leda Fulford, from Homicide Division," she said. "I'm sorry to bust in on you this way, but I'm looking for information on Percy Guildford, your neighbor."

Walpole looked at his wife in a peculiar way. "Why don't you sit down, have a cup of coffee," he said.

Jenny nodded. "I've got some made up in the kitchen. I'll be right back."

As she left the room, Walpole said, "Has homicide got a beef with Guildford?"

"Not really," Fulford said. "He just popped up on a list of people who might help us with a murder case."

"I don't know how he got on your list," Walpole said, "but I assure you, without knowing the details of your murder investigation, he won't be of much help to you."

Jenny Walpole returned with a tray and a beaker of coffee. Nothing was said as she poured coffee for everyone.

Fulford spoke out of curiosity, "How can you be so sure Guildford won't be able to help us?"

"Because," Walpole said, "he was an agent with the Division of Alcohol, Tobacco, and Firearms. Three weeks ago, he was seriously wounded in a battle with a gang of dope pushers holed up in a crack house. Yesterday, he died."

Fulford could not restrain an exclamation of surprise. "I'm flabbergasted. We thought Guildford might turn out to be a suspect. Now, I learn he's a law officer."

"Was," Walpole corrected.

"Yeah," Fulford said, shaking her head in disbelief. "Was!"

She thanked the Walpoles for the coffee and took her leave. ATF agents, she decided as she drove back to the station, should be better screened for political correctness toward women. And maybe they ought to get better combat training.

"It turns my stomach," Fulford said. She was thinking about the murder and sodomizing of Donovan Grey, thoughts that filled her mind with horror. "How do people get so vile? Are they just born wicked, or what?"

"A lot of people would agree with the born wicked theory. According to the Old Testament, everybody's born depraved. This guy, whoever he is, has probably been weird since birth."

"I guess it doesn't matter how he got that way. He's a beast and has to be caught."

"Amen. So far, however, we haven't got a viable suspect."

He told her about his visit with Simba and Kim. "If I use my imagination, I might make something of the fact that Hamlet rejects a covert invitation from Simba, who has a voluptuous body and is full of life, but turns around and puts the make on Kim, who is anorexic, or near it, and looks as if she's at death's door. Could he imagine Kim a living corpse?"

Fulford laughed. "That would make him a closet necrophiliac, wouldn't it? If we're going to use that kind of reasoning, I could declare Garner Jakes a potential necrophiliac because, as an undertaker, he has to be 'intimate' with dead bodies. I don't have any other reason to suspect him."

They were silent for a while, each thinking they should have prevented the violence to Donovan Grey. Each was nagged by the frustration that sprang from their inability to catch his killer.

Davis's eyes strayed frequently to the face and form of his companion. Her image fascinated him. For some time, he had been aware of his infatuation with her. She evoked yearnings he had not felt since his wife was killed, and he sensed she was, to some imponderable degree, attracted to him. "Leda," he said tentatively, "if I asked you to go out with me, would you do it?"

Her smile was encouraging. "Depends on where we go, Wade," she said, teasing him. "I don't think I'd like to go to a prize fight."

"I had dinner and a play at the Alliance Theater in mind. If that would suit you."

"Sounds good. I'm willing to give it a try. What's the play?"

"It's a revival of Harvey Fierstein's *Torch Song Trilogy.* Know anything about it?"

"I seem to remember reading a review of it several years ago. It's about gay men, isn't it?"

"Yes. Fierstein's gay. He wants to convince his audience that gays can love one another with the same devotion and fidelity as straights."

"I'd like to see it—with you." She put her hand on his and gave it a gentle squeeze.

"I'm glad," he replied.

Exactly how glad, he lacked words to say. Had she refused, his self-esteem would have plummeted into the cellar.

Chapter Seven

His phone rang at five-fifteen that evening. The voice identified itself as that of Garner Jakes. Davis was startled. His mind leaped in anticipation of important news.

"Yes, Mr. Jakes. How can I help you?"

There was a moment of hesitation, then Jakes said, "I read in the paper you're trying to identify a human arm found in the Chattahoochee. Perhaps I can help you." Again there was that slight hesitation. "I'm not sure. I think I can guess where the arm came from."

"Mr. Jakes," Davis replied, "we've found the woman's body from which the arm was cut. Do you think you can identify her also?"

Jakes seemed surprised. "Where did you find her? I've heard nothing about a body being found."

"The papers haven't yet gotten the story. She was found next to Proctor Creek, near the Chattahoochee."

"I'm surprised at the location," Jakes said, "but it's possible I can identify her. More than possible, really."

"Could you come down and look at her now?"

"There's something I have to do this evening. Would tomorrow morning be all right?"

"Mr. Jakes, identifying this woman is of the highest priority to us. Could you possibly make it this evening, even quite late if necessary?"

"I'm meeting someone who can confirm my guess as to this woman's identity. When I'm finished, I will come by the station. Don't expect me before eleven o'clock, however."

Davis was reluctant to wait but saw no reason to insist on Jakes appearing before he was willing to come.

"I'll be waiting," he said.

He called Fulford, told her of Jakes's call, and invited her to wait with him for Jakes to appear. "I'll treat you to a hamburger and french fries if you do," he promised.

"You don't need to bribe me, Wade. I'm eager."

They decided to have pizza instead of hamburgers. They dawdled over their meal at Benson's.

They could not help but speculate on how Garner Jakes could know who the woman was.

"He's an undertaker," Fulford said. "Maybe he officiated at her burial and now recognizes her."

"How?" Davis said. "He hasn't seen the body. He's got to have some other reason for thinking he knows her."

"Maybe he knows the person who stole her body. Maybe he's wrung a confession out of him."

"We'll have to wait and see, won't we?" Davis replied. He paused, a look of distaste on his face. "Let's not have any more shop talk. If I think too much about this case, I won't be able to finish my meal."

"Okay. So, seen any good movies lately?"

"*Death and the Maiden*. It's not so recent, but I liked it a lot. Did you see it?"

"No. What's it about?" Fulford asked.

"Pretty grim story. I'm afraid I made a bad choice for table talk."

"You can't back out now, Wade. My curiosity demands satisfaction."

"It's about a concentration camp survivor, a woman, who was raped and tortured. The war is over. She's married. Her husband is chairman of a commission on war crimes. He gets a visitor one night whom he receives in their living room, while she remains in the bedroom. She hears the visitor's voice and recognizes it as that of one of the men who raped her repeatedly. She disables his car so he cannot run away and then confronts him. The remainder of the movie involves her determination to convince her husband that this man is a war criminal, and to force the man to confess to raping her. She succeeds by displaying superior moral force and fierce determination."

"Not a nice story," Fulford said. "Why does it appeal to you?"

"Because I'm a crime fighter, I guess. And because I like to see good triumph over evil."

"I think there's more to it, Wade, than you're willing to admit. I think men use movies like that to work out their collective guilt about the fact that women in our society are viewed as nothing but instruments for male sexual gratification."

"Oh, come on, Leda. You don't really believe that, do you?"

"Of course I do. In the back of your mind, at this minute, you're suppressing your contempt for men because you see, in the man who raped that young woman's body and killed Donovan Grey, every man's sexual appetite for women run amok."

"Whew! I never should have raised the subject. Let me say one thing, though. As a male, I don't feel guilty because some men treat women as if they were made solely for their sexual gratification. Not all men are alike, you know."

"Okay, I'll let you off the hook. In the future, however, be careful not to get me started on man's inhumanity to women."

Davis stirred his coffee and stared at his companion, aware of the strong emotion that was gripping her. "What is it, Leda?" he asked.

"Just a memory, Wade. I don't know why I should confide in you. I've known you just a few weeks. Not long enough to really tell if you're what you appear to be—a decent guy. But I'll tell you anyway.

"Three years ago, when I was a senior at the university, my roommate, a beautiful, sensitive, innocent young woman was gang raped by four members of the football team. She reported the rape to the police, and the four were arrested. They were tried and convicted. In the process, the defense attorney tried to make out my friend was a woman of loose morals who actually provoked the rape. The judge was sympathetic to the defendants, calling them mere boys who did not understand the seriousness of their prank. They were sent to prison for two years and put on probation for eighteen months.

"My roommate's punishment was more severe. She dropped out of college and became a virtual recluse. She was emotionally devastated. She visits a psychiatrist regularly and has never been able to get her act together. Perhaps you can understand why, when I hear how some poor woman has been victimized, I get upset."

She paused, smiled at him, and said, "By the way, I didn't mean that any of the bad stuff I've said about men applies to you."

He understood her rage and shared it. He had been unaware until this moment how disquieting to both of them the investigation of this crime, this horrible offense against a woman, had been.

"Leda," he said, with a mind toward easing her rage, "we're going to catch Donovan Grey's murderer. I promise you that. We'll see he gets the punishment he deserves."

They sat quietly, faces sober, neither eager to pursue the topic. It came to life again with the arrival of Albert Saffron, who, uninvited, plumped down beside them like the first tremor of slipping tectonic plates.

"Don't you two ever go home? You know what all work and no play does to you. You look like something the cat dragged in."

"Thanks for the compliment," Davis said. You're a sorry-looking specimen yourself. No cat could drag you in, though. It would take a velociraptor to do the job."

"Congratulation, Wade," Saffron said amiably, enjoying the word-play. "Your insults are improving. But you rely too heavily on gross exaggeration. A light touch works better. 'Belly up to the table, sir, or would that put you out of earshot?' Now that's an insult worthy of an Academy Award."

He bit off a huge chunk of pizza, and, as he chewed it with evident relish, he looked at his companions for approval.

Fulford smiled in appreciation but then said seriously, "I don't understand, Albert, why you put up with the barbs people toss at you? Why don't you fight back?"

"They're good-natured people, Leda. They mean no harm. Besides, I'm planning to turn their insolence into income. I'm compiling a book of fat-man jokes. I even have a publisher interested. One of these days I'll land on the best-seller list."

"I'll be the first to buy a copy," Davis said. "Suitably autographed by the author, of course."

Davis admired Albert. Under the severest provocation, Albert never lost his temper or countered impertinence with rudeness. His usual flippancy hid an astute intellect and a deep reverence for the law. He had, on more than one occasion, as in the case of the Oaks Hospice killings, given Davis valuable advice in the analysis of evidence.

Fulford, apparently not to be outdone by Davis, said, "Put a copy of that book on reserve for me, Albert. I'll be eager to read it."

Albert smiled with pleasure. "You have my word. You get the first copies to roll off the press. Gratis."

He became aware of the tension shown by his friends. Assuming it had to do with their investigation, he asked, "How are you making out with the case of the nefarious necrophiliac?"

"The alliteration is appealing," Davis said, "but I prefer to call it the case of the butcher bird, the bird Donnie was so captivated by. Cutting off arms, impaling people—that's butchery, isn't it?"

"I won't argue the point," Albert said. "I'd like to know if you've made any progress."

"We're waiting for what could be a real break," Davis said. "We got a call from an undertaker named Garner Jakes who says he can identify the body of our armless girl. He's promised to get back to us late this evening."

Albert shook his head in disbelief. "You mean you let him put you off? Why didn't you insist he come in at once?"

"He said he was meeting someone who could confirm his guess as to the victim's identity. We gave him our cellular number, and he promised to call the minute he was free."

Albert expressed grave doubts. "Suppose something happens to him at that meeting. Suppose he is unable to confirm the girl's identity and changes his mind. If it were me, I'd call the guy right now and insist on him coming down here at once."

"I'm not as concerned as you are," Fulford said. "But I'll give him a ring."

She pressed his number and listened for the bell. After six rings, a voice from the machine said, "This is Garner Jakes. I'm sorry I can't answer the phone right now, but if you leave your name and number, I'll get back to you as soon as possible."

She identified herself and urged Jakes to contact the police the minute he got home.

Albert was somewhat mollified but still wore a worried expression. "If he's not home now, where the devil is he? He could be anywhere, and you've no way of locating him. Suppose he just disappears. You've lost the chance to identify the girl's body because you didn't insist he show up at once."

"Stop it, Albert," Davis said irritably. "A Monday morning quarterback is always smarter than the coach."

Albert appeared contrite. To Davis, however, his contrition was just that—appearance. He knew Albert had great faith in his own judgment. Seldom was he willing to retreat from a position he considered well-founded in deference to another's opinion.

"Look, I was only trying to help," he said.

He dropped the subject. "What else has happened besides Jakes's call?"

"We contacted a specialist in abnormal psychology, a Dr. Zorn, who gave us a profile of a necrophiliac. The profile was nothing more than an after-the-fact description drawn from a few clinical cases. It's almost useless."

"Don't despair. I've found something that may be useful," Albert said. "I was surfing the net a couple of days ago for information on necrophilia, and I came up with a journal article concerning the treatment of perpetrators of sexual violence and necrophilia. According to the blurb accompanying the citation, it relates sexual arousal to hormone levels, substance abuse, and social factors. It's in the Southeastern U. library. Sounds like a fun read."

"I can't wait to get my hands on it," Fulford said. "After what I've read about homosexuality being genetically determined, I wouldn't be surprised to read that necrophilia is the result of a wayward gene. If it were, punishment would be futile."

"Don't be cynical," Albert said, raising his vast bulk from the chair. "Quit speculating. Go find Garner Jakes. I sure hope you can."

When Albert had gone, Davis mulled over in his mind the significance of Jakes's absence. He had assumed that the meeting Jakes spoke about would take place in his home. Fulford's call, however, established the fact he was not there, and, as Albert had reminded them, they had no idea where he could be found. Their only alternative, it seemed, was to wait for him to call.

It was midnight. The disconsolate detectives looked at one another apprehensively. If something happened to Jakes that prevented him from contacting them, they faced a serious hitch in the progress of their case. They realized now, more acutely than ever before, how important it was for them to identify the body of the young woman found near Proctor Creek. Jakes had been certain he knew who she was. If Jakes were prevented from making that identification, they would have to resort to media publicity, something Davis did not want to do.

Davis rang Jakes's home again and received an invitation to leave his name and number from the answering machine. Jakes's mechanical voice roused a sense of foreboding deep within Davis's mind.

He turned, concern etched in his face, and said to Fulford, "I've got a bad feeling about this. Let's go over to his place. If he's still not there, we'll wait. He has to show up soon."

The house, located about three blocks from Jakes's mortuary, in a subdivision of modest homes, lay at the end of a cul-de-sac, dimly lighted by a fading streetlight. A small one-story structure, it had a one-car garage connected to the house by a walkway. The garage door was open. A green two-door sedan was parked inside.

"Did you by any chance see what kind of car Jakes drove when you were nosing around?" Davis asked.

"Yeah. A green compact. But I wouldn't infer anything from the fact that it's here. He could have been picked up by someone."

"True, but it's also possible he's inside."

"I don't see any lights."

"I don't either, but let's knock on the door anyway."

They mounted the steps, pounded on the door, then rang the bell. There was no response. Davis hammered hard on the door once more and called out Jakes's name. No sound came from within. He tried to open the door. It was locked.

"I have this irrational feeling Jakes is inside," he said to Fulford.

"Add my unfounded conviction to yours," she replied. "Why don't we try the back door?"

The screened porch in back was open. They went in and tried the back door. It was unlatched. They turned the knob and swung the door wide. When Davis turned on the light, they realized they were in the kitchen. Neat and well kept, the room showed nothing amiss.

"That must be the living room," Fulford said, pointing to a door to the left of the kitchen. When they went through it, they found themselves in a dining room, but through a door beyond, they could dimly see a television set and a small entertainment center. The living room. It was in this room that they found Jakes.

When Davis flipped the light switch on, what they saw was grotesque, a scene so bizarre as to be shocking. Jakes lay on his back in front of the sofa. A sword, which to Davis appeared to be of the Japanese ceremonial kind, had been thrust through his chest into the floor beneath, pinning him down like an insect in a collector's box. His hands, lacerated and bloody, showed he had not died at once but remained conscious long enough to try to dislodge the blade that transfixed him.

The two detectives stared at the grisly scene in morbid fascination, unable to break the sense of horror that had fallen upon them. Davis was the first to rouse himself.

"Leda, call forensics, will you? And the medical examiner."

As she complied, Fulford's eyes roved about the room and fastened upon two ornate fittings on the wall just over the sofa. Behind them, a faint, ghostly image was discernible.

"Look here, Wade. Over the sofa," she said. "That's where the sword came from. It was Jakes's own."

Davis, after examining the wall, agreed. "There's no mistaking it. The sword was his."

"Which means," Fulford said, "his murderer found it a weapon of opportunity, or he knew it was there all along and planned to use it to kill Jakes."

"It has to be the latter," Davis said. "Here's how I see it. I'm guessing a bit, but I can think of no other explanation that fits the facts as well. The murderer learned Jakes was going to identify the body. Perhaps Jakes told him. At any rate, the revelation would, for some reason, have put the murderer in peril, so he arranged to meet Jakes in his home and came prepared to use the sword he knew hung on the wall."

"I'll buy your scenario that far," Fulford said. "What I can't understand, though, is how the murderer persuaded Jakes to lie down on his back and remain there quietly while he plunged the blade into his chest."

"Unless I'm mistaken, the explanation for that," Davis said, "is right here on the coffee table."

Fulford saw two cups with saucers on the table.

"Those cups tell me that Jakes entertained a visitor, someone he knew well enough to break bread with, to use an original expression. Furthermore, I'm willing to bet the forensics people will find a sedative in one of those cups, probably sodium pentathol, the classic knockout potion."

"That has to be the answer," Fulford said. "If there are any fingerprints on those cups, we'll have a direct line to the killer."

"I doubt if we'll find any," Davis said. "We're dealing with a smart man. He'll be sure to have wiped his cup clean."

As they pursued their reconstruction of events, Chris McCalmon and a crew of forensic experts arrived and began to examine the scene. As McCalmon knelt by the body, the forensics people began photographing, measuring, taping, calculating angles, vacuuming the carpet and sofa, dusting for fingerprints, and doing all of this with such professional disinterest one would have thought they were accustomed to the sight of a man pinned to the floor with a ceremonial sword.

Chris McCalmon was not so unmoved. "Jesus, Wade, you and Leda seem to find more than your share of butchered bodies. First you discover a kid impaled on a bamboo stick; now you've got a guy pinned to the floor with a sword. What's your secret?"

"Just luck, I guess. Any idea how long he's been dead?"

"Judging from his temperature, I'd say four hours, maybe five."

Fulford looked at Davis. He nodded as she said, "Exactly the time we were eating at Benson's."

"Yes. And just as Albert was telling us we made a mistake for not insisting Jakes come in at once. Well," he added defensively, "I'm not going to lose any sleep over it. How could we have known which way the ball would bounce?"

In spite of his attempt to vindicate himself, Davis was overwhelmed by a sense of having been badly remiss. He should have insisted Jakes identify the body at once. He could have taken a car, gone to Jakes's place, and driven him to the morgue despite his objections. His failure to follow that course had resulted in Jakes's death and a missed opportunity to identify the girl's body. He was now back to square one in the investigation of Donovan Grey's murder, and, even worse, a new murder investigation had fallen into his lap.

Fulford, noting his dispirited look and slumped shoulders, said, "I don't think we could have foreseen what would happen to Jakes. We're not oracles. So let's not go on a guilt trip."

She looked around at the crew diligently combing the scene for clues. She saw that McCalmon had given the morgue workers an okay to remove the body. A gloved medic carefully worked the sword loose from the floor, withdrew it from Jakes's chest, handed it to one of the forensic crew, and began unzipping a body bag.

Fulford turned to Davis. "Look, haven't we had enough of this? We can't do anything more here. Let's go home and get some sleep."

Davis agreed. As they made for the door, Chris McCalmon called out, "I'll do the autopsy at eight in the morning, in case you'd like to watch."

"Thanks for the invitation," Davis responded. "I hate to decline your hospitality again. But I'm going to."

He had seen McCalmon at work before and had no wish to see him perform again. After making an incision from pubis to throat, Chris could, with a single hard tug and a quick slash of the scalpel, spill out a corpse's insides upon the table in one coherent mass. A sight to delight the eye.

Davis and Fulford, as if by previous agreement rather than happenstance, arrived in the office the next morning at ten. Neither looked or felt refreshed by fitful sleep.

"Can you stand another cup of coffee?" Davis asked. Without waiting for an answer, he went to the machine, fed in coins, and carried two cups back to his desk. They drank in silence for several minutes.

Then Davis asked, "Are you thinking what I'm thinking, that the person who murdered Jakes is the guy who murdered Donnie?"

"He has to be. Donnie was murdered because he saw the man who carried the girl's body to Proctor Creek and perhaps saw him begin to dismember her. Donnie fled before he could be harmed. The murderer then lured him back to the creek with the alleged sighting of a rare woodpecker and killed him."

"You can see an almost identical modus operandi in the case of Jakes," Davis said. "Jakes becomes a threat to the murderer by telling the police he could identify the body. Why her identification is a threat, I don't know, but it has to be the motive for the killing. When he learns what Jakes intends to do, he makes a date with him on some pretext, drugs him, and stabs him with the sword. Threat removed."

Fulford took a sip of coffee and shook her head. "Jakes had to be a threat to the murderer for some reason other than the mere identification of the body. The murderer is not stupid. He knows we'll eventually find out who the girl is, or was, so he became alarmed by something else that Jakes intended to tell us."

"I suppose you're right," Davis admitted. "Too bad we'll never know what it was."

The phone rang. Davis picked up the receiver, listened for several minutes, and then said, "Thanks, Chris. Let me have a written report when you can."

He hung up the phone and turned to Fulford.

"That was Chris with the autopsy results. As we suspected, Jakes had sodium pentathol in his system, not a lot, but enough to put him into a shallow slumber. The sword thrust almost missed the heart, but not quite. It slashed a small gash in the left ventricle so that, with each heartbeat, blood was spilled into the chest cavity. McCalmon thinks the shock of the sword going through his chest was enough to rouse Jakes from his drugged stupor. For maybe thirty seconds, he was conscious enough to try dislodging the weapon. The lacerated hands show he made a heroic effort."

Fulford shook her head in disbelief. "Poor bastard! What a terrible way to die."

Chapter Seven

The Great Hall of the Woodruff Arts Center reminded Davis of the Great Hall of the Kennedy Center in Washington, D.C. Not quite as spacious, the Woodruff Hall was, nevertheless, a hall to inspire respect. On the night of Davis's date with Fulford, it was thronged with well-dressed theater patrons and community leaders, many of whom were not regular patrons of the stage but attended to show their support for a worthy cause. Davis explained to Fulford that the performance of *Torch Song Trilogy* was a benefit for the Alliance and its experimental stage—a money-raising gala, held to supplement the theater's regular budget.

Most of the men wore evening clothes, garments that were, to the practiced eye, unquestionably expensive but conservatively tailored to avoid ostentation. Many of the younger men, being less inhibited, sported outfits of peacock splendor: jackets maroon or powder blue, shirts with lace cuffs and fronts, cummerbunds and bow ties of multicolored checks and whorls, trousers with vivid red stripes from cuff to waist.

The women, especially those who aspired to leadership in haute couture, wore elegant, strapless gowns that were cut in the back almost to the waist and deeply sloped in front so as to reveal their breasts in a provocative way.

Fulford, displaying an intuitive sense of good taste, wore a simple sheath that clung to her body like a second skin. Rust colored, with black lace around the hem and a black belt to match, it was adorned at the shoulder with an orchid Davis had been thoughtful enough to send. She drew admiring glances from eager young males.

Davis hoped he concealed his amorous interest in Fulford more successfully than some of her more blatant admirers, who ogled her without shame. She seemed unaware of the attention being paid her. Naivete or practiced indifference, Davis wondered. Fulford seemed enchanted with the milling crowd, her eyes moving from one cluster of noisy, gesticulating people to another.

"These, I take it, are Atlanta's beautiful people. The glitterati, or whatever, aren't they?" she asked Davis.

"I wouldn't call them beautiful," he replied, "but they do glitter. They're mostly well off, but some of them would be better described as blemishes on the city's image. I've met a few of them in connection with police business."

"Speaking of police business," she said, nodding to a clump of people off to their left, "isn't that our esteemed leader, Gerry Fillmore?"

"It is. As a prominent police figure, he likes to be seen among the movers and shakers. His interest in drama is about a minus five. My guess is Fierstein's play will rile him a bit. Can you imagine the great wave of sympathy that will wash over him when the playwright tells us that two gay men can be as devoted to one another, and as faithful, as a heterosexual couple?"

"Don't be mean, Wade. We're taking the night off, remember? Let the poor guy rub shoulders with his influential friends. Who knows, he may be doing the division some good."

Just then, the lights dimmed, and people began moving into the theater. Davis took Fulford's arm, and they joined the tide flowing into the auditorium.

The play was long, and during the two intermissions, Davis and Fulford shared their impressions.

"I'll buy Fierstein's notion that gay men are just as decent and vulnerable as straights," Fulford said. "But that scene in the rear of the gay bar with men making love in the dark, not caring who their partner is, turned me off."

"It does that to most people," Davis said. "I've heard Fierstein's sorry he wrote it in. If he had it to do over again, he'd leave it out."

"He should," Fulford said. "It puts too much emphasis on sex. People can be sympathetic toward gays, if they don't think too much about the way they have sex. Sex is only a small part of gay life, just as it is for straights. We don't judge straight people by the way they satisfy their sex urges. We look at a straight man and we think, 'He's a banker, or a doctor, or a scientist.' We don't think about his sexual preference."

"Yes, but people have always labeled sexual behaviors as right or wrong. For centuries, anal sex was considered wrong, immoral.

Remember what God did to the people of Sodom. That attitude is changing, but slowly. Gay bashing is still common. But a lot of people now try to be nonjudgmental, to accept homosexuality as an alternative lifestyle. It's the politically correct thing to do."

"Do you think that's wrong?" Fulford asked.

"No, but I think it's hard for people to really mean it when they say it."

When the play was over, Davis invited Fulford to his apartment for a nightcap.

She accepted. She was curious to know more about the man who, although she had known him for a relatively short time, appealed to her strongly. From his colleagues, she had learned only a few sketchy facts. He was a widower, his wife having died in an auto accident two years ago. He was something of a loner. No one on the force considered him a close friend. He did not date, except on rare occasions, and appeared to have no significant other in his life. He liked music and legitimate theater. Those facts were enough to intrigue her, to whet her interest, to make her wish to know him better.

He fixed them a drink, a vodka and tonic for her, a bourbon and water for himself. They sat close to one another on the sofa, saying nothing, sipping their drinks.

After a while, Davis said, "You're an attractive woman, Leda. I like you. Maybe like is an understatement."

"If like is an understatement," she said, her dark eyes resting on his face with a trace of amusement, "what would the proper non-understated word be?"

"Clever woman," Davis said. "I'm supposed to say love, right? Maybe someday I will. I'm not sure I'm ready to say it yet."

"Well then, how about adore? Idolize?"

"Will you settle for desire? I have to admit, Leda, when I asked you here, I hoped we might end up making love. Now I find I haven't the slightest idea of how to promote that wish. Should I plead for your favor in piteous tones? Should I fling my arms around you, cover you with kisses, and tell you how wonderful you are?"

Fulford was not naive. She had understood from the beginning that Davis might want to make love to her, and she admitted to herself that, when she agreed to go to his apartment, the thought of having sex with him had been in the back of her mind. Now she was feeling a sense of welling desire.

She put her hand on his and gave it a gentle squeeze. "I like you, too, Wade. But we're moving pretty fast, don't you think? We've known each other just a few weeks, and this is our first date. My mama drilled a little rhyme into my head when I was a teenager. It went like this: 'Nice girls on their first date, never, never fornicate.' If I jump in the sack with you, maybe I won't find the experience a fate worse than death, but I'm a nice girl, Wade. I hope you understand."

Davis was stricken. "Leda, I'm not a bad guy. Did I come across as an overeager lecher? I didn't mean to. Do you want me to take me home?"

He looked so hurt she felt sorry for him. "Could I have another drink before I go?"

His face showed hope reborn. "I'll fix it."

When he handed her the drink, she said, "A woman likes to feel she's desirable for more than sex. Are you eager to make love to me just because I've got a good body and a nice face?"

"No. It's more than that," he said in a serious tone. "You're a good cop. You've got brains. I like your sense of humor. I like the way you look at me when I've done something stupid. I like the way you make me feel alive." He paused, looking at her affectionately. "The list is long. Shall I go on?"

"Someday I want to hear the whole thing. Not now. Now, I want you to put your arms around me and give me a kiss."

Her mouth was warm, sensuous. Her lips were apart, her tongue exploring. He could feel her firm breasts against him. He undid the zipper of her dress and let it fall about her feet. Then he picked her up and carried her into the bedroom.

"I wasn't going to do this," she said, as she finished undressing. "I was going to be a good girl."

As he slipped in bed beside her and let his hands move gently over the contours of her body, he said huskily, "You *are* a good girl, Leda. You could never be anything else. That's why I love you."

After that memorable night, Davis could not refrain from touching her. He would let his hand briefly cover hers when they sat together at lunch; when they stood up, he guided her by the elbow toward the door; when he helped her with her coat, his arm lingered on her shoulder a trifle longer than necessary.

Fulford discouraged him. "Don't do things like that, Wade. People are bound to notice. They'll read more into your behavior than I'm comfortable with."

"I don't care what people think," Davis replied. "I have to express my feelings, don't I?"

A week later, when they met Albert Saffron at the coffee machine, Davis's behavior was restrained but still too familiar. Albert, eyeing the two with amusement, made a casual observation.

"Your secret is safe with me."

The remark startled Davis. "What secret, Albert? What are you talking about?"

"You know what I'm talking about, Wade. And so do you, Leda. The relationship between the two of you has evolved from a purely professional one into something deeper and richer. To put it bluntly, the two of you are shacking up."

"I rather like the first version, Albert," Fulford said. "It's not so crude."

Davis was upset. "Are we really that obvious?"

"Leda's pretty restrained. But you, Wade, you're all over her."

Thereafter, Davis was more circumspect. He managed to treat Fulford with a formality sufficient to conceal his emotional attachment. She, having been less demonstrative, had little difficulty keeping her distance.

Within a few days, Davis grew tired of the restraint and said to Fulford, "Let's quit this hiding-our-feelings business. I want you to move into my apartment. I've got plenty of room. Let everyone know where we stand."

"Where *do* we stand?" Fulford asked. "I haven't worked that out yet, Wade. You seem to think I've made a permanent commitment to you. I haven't. I haven't known you long enough. I admit you seem like the right guy, but I can't be sure. And you don't know me all that well. I might be a regular bitch when I let my guard down."

"I can't believe that. And I can't believe you think I'm some sort of love 'em and leave 'em guy."

"Right now you're not. What about six months or a year from now? Will you still feel the same way about me? Let me tell you a little story. When I was a junior in college, I was invited to a party. There I met a famous football player, a sure national trophy winner. He asked me for a date, and when we went out together, I went to bed with him. He asked me to live with him, share his apartment. I was so flattered, I almost knocked myself out moving furniture. He told me he loved me in a way he had never loved anyone before, that he would never look at another woman. I bought it all—hook, line, and sinker.

"I went off on Christmas vacation. When I came back, I caught him in bed with a blonde cheerleader. She was a tramp. They say the coaching staff used her as an inducement to recruit prospective players. The hurt was intense."

She paused, looking at Davis for understanding.

"Are you putting me in the same league with the football player, a guy who had been spoiled rotten by media attention?"

"Of course not. All I'm saying is, don't form an alliance in haste."

"Okay," he said, resentment in his voice. "If that's the way it is, that's the way it is."

He turned and left the room.

Chapter Eight

They were going through Garner Jakes's house on the off chance they might find something that would link him to his assailant. It was boring work, made more tiresome by small expectations. Rummaging through his closets, desk, books, wastebasket, and list of frequently called phone numbers, they found nothing.

"He must have had a family," Davis said. "A mother, a father, brothers, sisters, some kind of kin. There's not a single entry in his phone log for any sort of relative."

"Probably wouldn't need to write such numbers down," Fulford said. "He'd have numbers like that memorized."

"Well, it's clear we're doing no good here; let's try our luck at the mortuary."

The inside of the mortuary, a spartan place at best, shone bleakly under the fluorescent lights, whose stark rays gave the room a garish, enameled glow. Not very tasteful for a mortuary, Davis thought.

About a dozen coffins sat about the room on gurney-like supports, lids open, velvet interiors proffering a last, luxurious resting place for the dead. Their well-fashioned and beautifully made lids and flanks contrasted sharply with the poorly designed and decorated room.

"I get the feeling," Davis said, "that Mr. Jakes had little money to waste on ambience."

"He'd been in business a little over a year," Fulford said. "Funny, isn't it? I'm sure he never thought he would join the ranks of his customers so soon."

Davis grunted in acknowledgment of his companion's remark. "I'm sure he wouldn't think it was funny."

"I didn't mean funny in the usual sense," Fulford said testily.

They were now in Jakes's small office, a modest rectangle wedged into one corner of the room. Davis was looking at an appointment book and a pile of letters on the desk while Fulford booted up the computer and began searching its contents.

Finding nothing noteworthy on the desk, Davis examined the framed certificates and diplomas hanging on the wall.

"Here's something interesting," he called out to Fulford. "Jakes got a degree, or a certificate I guess it is, from Cawthon's School of Burial Science. Quite a coincidence, wouldn't you say?"

Fulford, who seemingly enjoyed being nasty for the moment, said, "I don't know. How many schools of burial science are there in the area? I suspect he didn't have a very wide choice."

Davis grinned. "Okay, so it wasn't much of a coincidence. It at least suggests we should talk to Cawthon for background on Jakes."

They were silent for a while. Davis flipped through a Rolodex file, discovered the combination of a small office safe, and opened it. He found nothing but a few United States savings bonds of small denominations and a certificate of deposit on a local bank for the sum of three thousand dollars.

Suddenly, Fulford gave a low whistle. "I'm into his file of paid-in-advance burials. Ralph Hamlet has got one. The two must know each other, if only on a business level. That gives me an idea."

Her hand deftly maneuvered the mouse, pointed the arrow, and clicked. She moved the mouse over another icon and clicked again.

"Well, what do you know! Listen to this, Wade. Here's an e-mail letter to Jakes that says, 'Will Saturday evening at seven be okay?' It's signed Ralph H. Who do you suppose Ralph H. is?"

"Haven't the foggiest," Davis said, beaming like a man who had just won the lottery.

Ralph Hamlet ushered them into his living room, seated them on the sofa, and offered coffee. While he was brewing the drink, they examined the room with considerable interest. They had been prepared, from what Art Walker had told them of Hamlet's skill with stained glass, to see some unusual works. What they saw was little less than astonishing. First, there were several abstractions in the style, Fulford guessed, of Klee and Modigliani, whose works she had seen in a recent exhibit. Their colors seemed to grow out of the pattern so that shape and hue made a unified whole. Davis, who had little interest in or knowledge of abstract art, was forced to admit they were visually arresting and provocative.

The remaining works, about a dozen of them, were strictly traditional and realistic, but with a certain surreal quality, as if the artist had recollected them from a dream. A zebra's stripes seemed woven out of the foliage against which he stood. An egret, neck poised to strike an unwary fish, shimmered and undulated like a reflection on the water. A fish eagle, its prey clutched in tight-fisted talons, seemed about to emerge from the frame and soar about the room.

Fulford whispered softly, "I'd say the guy has quite a talent."

Davis nodded in agreement. "And a scholar to boot, according to Delbert Linn."

"We were admiring your glass work," he said, as Hamlet emerged from the kitchen bearing a tray with cups and a pot of coffee. "We're impressed."

"Thank you. It's quite good work, I agree. You'll note I do not suffer from false modesty." His smile was tinged with a slight cynicism.

"Nor should you be," Davis said. "The work speaks for itself. We did not come to see your work, however, gratifying as the exposure has been. We are investigating the murder of a man you know, Garner Jakes."

"Jakes has been murdered?" He seemed genuinely astonished. "I can't believe it. I saw him just a few days ago."

It happened last night. We are interviewing his friends and acquaintances. The more information we compile about a murdered person, the more likely we will find something pointing us to his assailant."

Hamlet nodded, as if Davis's statement were common knowledge. "I shall be as helpful as I can, but I didn't know the man well."

"His records indicate you bought a prepaid burial plan from him."

Hamlet made a little nod of disparagement. "I'm afraid I'm given to morbid anticipation. Fortunately, I bought the plan on an installment basis. I pay small quarterly amounts but haven't made many payments yet. I suppose I'll be out of pocket for those sums, now that he's dead."

"Perhaps not," Fulford said. "Someone will probably take over his business and honor his obligations."

Davis watched carefully for Hamlet's reaction as he said, "Detective Fulford found an e-mail letter in Jakes's computer, presumably making an appointment with you for next Saturday at seven."

Hamlet showed no surprise or concern. "Oh, that. He wanted to learn how to work with leaded glass. I offered to teach him some basics in return for credit against my prepaid burial contract. I used e-mail to set up practice sessions."

"I didn't see any glass or came in his home or at his place of business," Davis said.

"He wasn't far enough along to have a setup of his own. He worked in my studio in the evenings. Brought his own came and glass. He was having trouble learning to cut glass. A steady hand is required, but more important is a sense of confidence. This he lacked. The result was a clumsiness that resulted in a lot of waste. A few more sessions and he probably would have got the hang of it."

"Where's your studio?" Fulford asked, pretending ignorance.

"When I bought it, this house had a nuclear bomb shelter in the back yard. A previous owner, like so many people in the fifties and sixties, was apparently convinced nuclear war was inevitable. He built himself a concrete bunker guaranteed to withstand an atomic blast. I found the space useless until I conceived the idea of using it as a studio. Plenty of lights, a ventilation system, and an efficient dehumidifier was all it took."

"So your practice sessions with Jakes took place in the bunker?" Davis asked.

"They did. He was a bit claustrophobic at first. Said an undertaker was naturally averse to working in a vault. But we joked about it, calling it Jakes's crypt and things like that, and he quickly got over his phobia."

"Did he ever suggest he had enemies, anyone with whom he was at cross purposes?"

"Our conversations seldom dealt with personal matters. He mentioned some time ago that he and his father had a falling out. He didn't say why. I got the impression there was really bad blood between them. You don't think his father could have murdered him, do you?"

"No. But we'll want to talk to him."

"I suppose," Hamlet said with an air of resignation, "you'll want to know all about my private life." Then, without being prompted, he said, "There isn't much to tell. I was born to middle-class parents in Waycross. Went to high school there. I was the only member of my family to graduate from college and then go on to earn a Ph.D. degree, which I got, incidentally, from the University of Florida. I have been teaching, with some distinction I might add, here at Southeastern for the past twelve years."

"An enviable record," Fulford said, as Hamlet paused, scanning the faces of the detectives for reaction. "Just one or two more things and we'll be finished. You appear to be living here alone. You're not married?"

"My wife, whom I loved dearly, died a little over a year ago. Since then, I have not become interested in another woman."

"There is no need for us to pry into a sensitive area. If you'll just answer one more question. I assure you it's a formality. Please don't be offended. Where were you last night between seven and midnight?"

"Ah! You suspect I may have murdered Jakes. I'm flattered. I hate to disappoint you, but I had absolutely no reason to wish Jakes dead. He seemed a simple, unaffected man who, if I were to guess, didn't have an enemy in the world. As for my whereabouts last night, I cannot produce an alibi. I watched a news broadcast from seven to eight and then spent a couple of hours in my studio, working on a glass project. I went to bed around ten-thirty or eleven o'clock. I was alone the whole time."

"Well, sir, you're not really a suspect. As I said, the question was routine."

They thanked him for his cooperation and brought the interview to an end.

Within thirty minutes of leaving Hamlet, they sat in the office of Weldon Knowles, a colleague of Hamlet's at Southeastern. Davis was not satisfied with the image of Hamlet he had gotten when he inquired among his neighbors. The picture was shallow, probably because, having little to do with Hamlet, they saw only the surface of the man. Delbert Linn's information had been tainted by resentment of the police. Simba and Kim had offered a more detailed and perhaps a more reliable view. Davis hoped Knowles could expand on what he had previously learned.

Knowles, though polite, seemed reluctant to talk about his friend. Davis knew from experience that most people were reserved when asked by police officers, acting in an official capacity, for information about friends. He offered his standard assurances. His questions were merely routine. They cast no reflection upon the subject of the interrogation. He would treat all information as confidential.

Knowles finally agreed to speak candidly and to reveal all pertinent information.

Davis thanked him, asked a few innocuous questions, and then posed the question that really interested him.

"Did Hamlet ever date one of his students?"

Knowles seemed offended at the question. "I suppose you've been reading stories in the press alleging that male professors often coerce female students into sexual encounters by threatening them with poor grades. That's nonsense. Typical media sensationalism! I've never heard of a documented case occurring at Southeastern. While I admit such a thing might happen, it would be rare. The vast majority of professors are responsible people devoted to the welfare of their students."

He paused a moment, reflecting on the vehemence of his response.

"Do I protest too much?" he said diffidently. "I guess the implication that Ralph might have done such a thing set me off. The answer to your question is unequivocal. Ralph Hamlet would never have taken advantage of a female student. Period."

"You speak with a great deal of conviction," Fulford said. "Any particular reason for feeling so strongly?"

"Well, yes, there is. Ralph Hamlet is a man deeply in love. He is, was, I should say, married to a beautiful young woman whom he adored. Sadly, she died a year ago. Although she no longer lives, Ralph is still in love with her. He remains faithful to her memory. He would never look at another woman."

"But after a year," Davis said, "he might need the love of a real live woman."

"If Ralph's devotion to his wife were merely ordinary, I might agree. But there was nothing ordinary about it. He almost died of grief at her passing. He spent hours beside her coffin, unwilling to take his eyes from her. Friends, I among them, tried to console him, but he rejected our good offices.

"In some fashion, he found out about a California firm called Cryonics Incorporated. They freeze a loved one's body and store it in a glass case in a mausoleum, where it lies in view to be seen as family members wish. Ralph was determined to have his wife's body preserved in that fashion."

"Surely he didn't carry through with that plan," Fulford said.

"He would have, except for the intervention of his friends. Dean Folger and I argued so vehemently against his intention, he finally gave up and rejected the idea. You shouldn't think, because of this episode, Ralph is emotionally unstable. This whole business about the cryonics lasted just a few days and was the result of an emotional trauma devastating enough to unsettle anyone."

"We don't think that at all," Davis assured him. "When we interviewed him, we found him to be self-possessed and quite stable. I'd like to ask you about another matter concerning Professor Hamlet. He has a studio inside an atomic bomb shelter. Have you ever been there?"

"Of course, once or twice. Is there some particular thing you wish to know about it?"

"Is it just one big room?" Fulford asked.

"Actually, it's more elaborate than you would expect. There is a main room, which was intended, I suppose, as a combination living room–bedroom. There's a bathroom, a storage space for supplies which is separated from the main room by a folding door, and a kitchen nook with a sink and running water.

"You see, those places were intended to shelter people for several days, or weeks, in case of an atomic blast. We forget how fearful people were in those day. Hiroshima and Nagasaki were fresh in their minds. Seems a bit of an overreaction these days. Ralph has turned a white elephant into something quite useful."

"I vaguely remember the bomb shelter craze," Davis said. "I was just a kid, and, though our family never built one, we argued one of the hard questions of the day, 'Would you let your neighbors into your shelter if nuclear war began?' I often wonder what would have happened, given an actual blast, if someone died. Would they have just opened the door and chucked the body out?"

"They would have been afraid to do that," Knowles assured him. "Opening the door would have let in too much radiation. In Ralph's place, there's a kind of shelf dug into the earth behind the storage space, a shelf that's large enough to accommodate a couple of bodies if laid out horizontally. I don't know if it was intended for that purpose, but it would have served."

He paused, a look of distaste on his face. "We're getting awfully morbid, don't you think?"

Fulford nodded. "We are, indeed. I've just one more question. We've heard some of Hamlet's neighbors were upset with him for helping students defend a kind of commune they had set up in a rented house near his home. Did that create a serious flap, or was it just a minor thing?"

"Somewhere in between, I'd say. A few people were very angry, and Ralph got a couple of nasty phone calls. But in the main, people accepted the students after, at Ralph's insistence, they agreed to avoid loud music, wild parties, and sex orgies. A couple of the students—they were all women—got a crush on Ralph, out of gratitude, I believe. He handled the matter very circumspectly."

"Would one of those students have been a girl named Kim?"

"Kim Kendall, yes. She was attracted to Ralph, hung about after class and tried to engage him in conversation. She invited herself into his home, pretending she was vitally interested in his glasswork."

"Did he allow her to get away with that?" Davis asked.

"Just that one time, out of kindness."

"But there was never any intimacy between them?"

"None whatsoever. Ralph was relieved when her infatuation finally died."

Davis and Fulford, finding nothing further to inquire about, thanked Knowles for his cooperation and excused themselves. Knowles walked them to the door and promised, at their request, to say nothing to Hamlet about their visit.

Chapter Nine

When Chris McCalmon appeared for their date, Fulford was pleasantly surprised. She had never seen him dressed up before. On the job he always wore a white, ankle-length smock, full cut and voluminous enough to make him appear obese. He had not bothered, when working, to remove it, even at lunch. He preferred to eat from a brown bag at the desk in his lab. Now, as she opened the door to him, he appeared fashionable enough to be a model for a men's clothing designer.

"Well, look at you!" she said. "The very image of the modern medical examiner."

He laughed. "Ralph Lauren's best. Don't you know that clothes make the man?" He paused, looking at her appreciatively. "You don't look so bad yourself. What is that thing you're wearing?"

"That thing, sir," she said, pretending insult, "is a Demi Moore tuxedo. All-male jacket, all-female skirt, and black pantyhose. You like it?"

"I'm overwhelmed. You put Demi to shame."

"Flatterer. Do you want a drink before we go?"

"O'Brian's makes the best cocktails in Atlanta. Let's go test their reputation. We can dawdle over drinks as long as we like."

"Okay, I'm ready."

O'Brian's, dimly lighted, had walls whose decorations memorialized Irish culture—harps, stars, leprechauns, dancing Colleens, shamrocks, plows, and IRA gunmen. Waitresses wore Irish costumes and spoke with an exaggerated brogue.

"I think I may overdose on all this Irish stuff," Fulford said.

"A couple of drinks and you won't notice a thing."

So they ordered. Fulford wanted a margarita. McCalmon had a martini.

As they sipped their drinks, McCalmon said, "Tell me about you,

Leda. You're a stranger."

"I was born in one of Atlanta's better-class slums. My parents rose to middle-class affluence, if you can call it that, because both of them started working long hours at low pay, learned the ropes in their respective jobs, and eventually moved up the ladder. My dad became a Marta dispatcher, and my mom became an administrative assistant to the head of the Department of Business and Professional Regulations. My brother and I both went to college and got bachelor's degrees. He's now in law school. I went on and earned a master's degree in criminology. And here I am, consorting with famous lawmen."

"You're not calling me a famous lawman, are you? If you are, you're wrong. I haven't made my reputation yet. Not of the magnitude I would like. But one day I will. I began in poverty, too. My father deserted my mother the day I was born. She raised me by herself without welfare or assistance of any kind. You can imagine how she was forced to scrimp on housing, food, medicine, you name it. We survived, that's all."

"How did you manage to get an education?"

"I took a biology class in high school. My teacher, a Miss Reeder, thought I had the interest and ability to go to college. She unearthed a series of scholarships that took me through a bachelor's degree. Then came a minority grant and a staggering loan to get me through med. school. I still owe the government about thirty-five hundred dollars. I expect to pay that off by next spring."

Fulford looked at him, respect in her eyes. "I'm impressed, Chris. I never had to struggle the way you did. My parents earned enough to educate me without my having to worry."

"That's the kind to have," Chris said, a trace of envy in his voice. "But let's forget the past. The present calls for another round of drinks, don't you think?"

"One more, Chris. That's my limit. You know women don't metabolize alcohol as well as men."

When the drinks came, Fulford noticed with interest that Chris's martini had somehow become a double.

They ordered, at Chris's suggestion, O'Brian's famous Irish stew. Fulford had to admit, with her first taste, it lived up to its reputation.

"Best stew I've ever eaten," she told McCalmon. "How did you ever discover this place?"

"Serendipity," he said. "I did a post-mortem on a newspaper

restaurant reviewer. Found a card for O'Brian's in his pocket with a glowing recommendation. Unfortunately, he never got to publish it. Incidentally, he died of a heart attack. Four major arteries clogged. Been eating in the wrong places, I guess."

"Makes me feel good about this stew."

McCalmon was suddenly aware of his inapt comment. "Forgive me, Leda. I sometimes think of my job as ordinary, just as fit for dinnertime conversation as a computer programmer's or an auto mechanic's."

"You're forgiven."

They had finished their meal, and Chris was enjoying a brandy.

"Tell me about this cat show you're taking me to," Fulford said. "I didn't know you were a cat fancier."

"I'm not anymore. I used to have a Siamese. Beautiful blue eyes; sable face, tail tip, and paws; white snow over the rest of her. She almost died of loneliness. I was away all day, sometimes most of the night. She got anxious as hell when I left in the morning, and she went crazy when I came home at night. I had to give her up. I couldn't stand the emotional trauma I was putting her through."

Fulford heard the sadness in his voice and responded with sympathy, "I'm sure giving her up was painful, but you did the right thing. Don't cat shows bring back unhappy memories?"

"Not really. Shows like the one we're going to see let me enjoy cats without the responsibility of caring for one." He paused and looked at his watch. "Maybe we'd better go. It's after eight, and there are over two thousand cats in this show."

"We don't have to look at them all, do we?" Fulford asked with some alarm.

"No, but there are some forty-five or fifty breeds. You might want to see examples of each."

When they entered the Civic Center, Fulford was amazed at the display. Long aisles, with cages on each side, spanned the length of the auditorium. She guessed there were at least twenty such rows. Many of the cats were not in their cages but sat outside, calmly preening their fur and staring at the spectators. It appeared to Fulford that all of them eyed the spectators in a haughty, patronizing manner.

A cash bar had been set up to one side, and McCalmon invited her to have a drink. "I'll have a cola," she said, and he set off to get it. When he returned, he was sipping a drink from a small mason jar.

"What in the world is that?" she asked, looking at the jar.

"It's moonshine," he said. "Probably not the real stuff, but people buy it in jars like this in order to feel illicit. It adds a psychological boost to the kick, which is not inconsiderable." He grinned, raised the jar to her, and took a large gulp. He grimaced. "That's the way you're supposed to do it. It's a little much for me, though. I'm a born sipper."

He began playing tour guide. "This show is sponsored by the CFA, the Cat Fanciers Association, the largest association of its kind in the country. In each pedigree class, the judges pick a Champion, and the best of show, chosen from the Champions, is called the Grand Champion."

Fulford was listening with half an ear. Her attention was completely absorbed by the many distinctive and extraordinarily beautiful cats surrounding her.

"Look at this one," she said excitedly to McCalmon. The cat had light blue eyes and dusky white fur, but its ears, tail, and paws were dark brown, almost black.

"That's a seal point Siamese like the one I used to own," McCalmon said. "It's one of the most popular breeds in America." He stood there for a moment, looking at the cat wistfully. Fulford supposed him lost in sentimental reflection. "Did you know, Leda," he said after a long pause, "that female cats have a bifurcated uterus. It's Y-shaped, and in each arm of the Y, she can have as many as three kittens."

Fulford looked at him with surprise and a little amusement. "No, Chris, I didn't know anything about a cat's uterus. I'll file that away among useful, but not immediately relevant information."

McCalmon caught nothing unusual about her remark and went on with enthusiasm, "Over here is a Havana Brown. The color is called chestnut, but I call it chocolate brown. The breed was established when a black shorthair female was mated to a seal point Siamese."

Fulford nodded in acknowledgment but let her eyes rove to cats that were astonishingly unfamiliar. "What in the world is this one?" she asked McCalmon. The cat was almost naked. The very short hair of a pale brown hue that grew on its face, ears, paws, and tail resembled suede. When it sat on its haunches, the skin of its sides, belly, and shoulders wrinkled like crumpled paper.

"He's a Sphinx," McCalmon said. "It's an inbred mutation. Years ago there used to be another hairless variety called the Mexican hairless. One advantage to this cat—you don't have to worry about hairballs. You know about hairballs?"

Fulford shook her head with an expression suggesting she could live without knowing about hairballs. McCalmon failed to notice.

"Cats clean their fur by licking it. This causes them to swallow hair, which eventually forms a ball in the cat's stomach. They have to vomit it up. Cats vomit easily."

Fulford gave him a tolerant look. "That's really interesting, Chris. I don't suppose I'd ever have known about hairballs if it hadn't been for this show."

McCalmon smiled. "You never get too old to learn, do you? I think I'll have another one of these." He gestured with his mason jar. "You want another cola?"

"I think I'll coast."

When he returned, Fulford was admiring a marble-colored Manx. "I never knew there were cats without tails," she said. "Is this a new breed?"

McCalmon loosened his collar, took off his jacket, and hung it over his arm. "Getting warm in here, don't you think? No, the Manx is an old breed. There's a story about how it lost its tail that goes clear back to the Bible. It seems a couple of tardy cats almost failed to get aboard Noah's Ark. Noah had the door almost shut when they squeezed in. Unfortunately, the door caught their tails before they could get fully inside and nipped them off."

"That's a cute story, Chris." She looked at her companion with concern. His face was flushed, and sweat stood out on his brow. "Are you all right?"

"A bit woozy," McCalmon admitted. "Do you suppose I drank too much of that moonshine?"

"Could be," she said, concern in her voice. She made a quick decision. "I think we'd better go, don't you? I also think I'd better drive."

McCalmon made no objection. He handed her the keys and slumped down in the front seat of the car beside her. By the time they reached his apartment, he was asleep. She shook him, and he woke up briefly, long enough to make it up the stairs, with her help, and into the living room. She settled him on the sofa, put a pillow under his head, and removed his shoes. He opened his eyes briefly and muttered a word that sounded like "Sorry."

She kissed his forehead gently, opened the door, looked back to make sure he was all right, and made her way out to the street.

The next morning, her phone rang at seven. It was Chris.

"First of all," he said, "I don't drink."

Fulford laughed. "You sure gave a good imitation of it last night."

"I know. I was nervous about the impression I would make on you. Very nervous. So I thought a little alcohol would calm me down. At first it worked beautifully. I was as cool as a cucumber."

"You were very charming, very smooth."

"Then I blew it. I went too far."

"You were the calmest, coolest person I ever saw, Chris. In fact, you were so composed, I had a hard time getting you up the stairs."

"Leda, please. Don't rub it in. I'm knee-deep in guilt as it is. Will you forgive me?"

"Maybe."

"Maybe? How about yes?"

"Will you give up the booze next time?"

"I was never on it. I promise. An easy promise to keep."

"Okay. How's your head?"

"It's there. I can feel it."

"Take a couple of aspirin and call me tomorrow."

Chapter Ten

At Fillmore's request, they met for a progress report. When Davis tried to summarize the case, he realized how little had been accomplished. The young woman's body still had not been identified. That was his fault for opposing the publication of her picture in the media. His opposition now seemed demonstrably unwarranted.

"The M.E. reported Donovan Grey died from a blow to the back of his head," he told Fillmore, "probably with something like a heavy crescent wrench, the kind of thing a man might carry in a pickup truck. The weapon has not been found. Grey was dead when he was impaled on the bamboo shaft. He had been sodomized. Forensics has DNA samples from the semen, which should be useful if we ever lay a hand on the culprit."

"What about fingerprints?"

"None. The guy obviously wore gloves. There were signs a small truck had been parked about twenty yards from the scene. Foliage crushed and a few drops of oil. Some paint was lifted from thorns that appear to have scraped the side of a vehicle."

"Nothing else?"

"Underbrush was crushed down, but there were no useful footprints. Fibers were found clinging to the underbrush. They were from a sweater. Not the victim's."

Fillmore looked unhappy. "This undertaker, Jakes, why didn't you insist he identify the girl's body at once?"

Davis was contrite. "In hindsight, I should have. But he asked for a few hours delay while he kept a previously arranged appointment. He said he wanted to confirm the woman's identity. I didn't see any point in being hard-nosed about it. After all, the guy volunteered to help us. How was I to know he would get himself killed?"

Fillmore shook his head sagely. "The first rule of good detective work is to seize the moment. You know that."

Davis said nothing. He looked at Fulford, a frustrated expression on his face.

"You needn't tell me the details of Jakes's murder," Fillmore said. "I've read the report. What has forensics found?"

"Not much," Davis said. "It's clear the murderer wore gloves. They found powder on the handle of the sword, the kind of powder dusted on latex gloves to make them easy to put on. They think the gloves were probably the kind used in hospitals or dentists' offices.

"There were two cups on the coffee table containing the residue of instant coffee. In one of them, Jakes's we assume, traces of sodium pentathol were found. No hairs, fibers, or other debris turned up."

Fillmore, who had been listening carefully and making notes on a memo pad, said, "The business of the gloves is interesting. I know it's stretching reason a bit far, but are we warranted in believing the murderer might have been, I stress might have been, a doctor or a dentist?"

Fulford nodded. "Or another undertaker. They use gloves of that kind, too."

Davis said nothing, but he remained skeptical. Latex gloves of the kind they were talking about could be purchased in any drugstore or crafts shop in the city.

"I trust you'll explore the avenues suggested by the gloves," Fillmore said, in a tone that indicated the statement was not an advisory but an order. "And speaking of possibilities, does it strike you that the person who murdered Jakes is probably the same person who murdered Donovan Grey?"

Fulford, who had been reluctant to speak before, now said, "On the face of it, it seems obvious. The only hitch, however, is motive. The man who killed Grey did so because he feared Grey would finger him as the person who dumped our nameless girl's body at Proctor Creek. But Jakes was killed, presumably, because the murderer didn't want him to identify the body. That doesn't make much sense. He must have had another reason we don't know about."

Fillmore thought that over. "Any idea what his reason might have been?"

"If Jakes knew who the girl was, he probably also knew who had taken her from her grave and sexually molested her. I'm sure he intended to tell us who that person was. Unfortunately, he let the murderer know his intention and was silenced."

Looking down at the notes on his closely written memo pad, Fillmore nodded in agreement. "I hope you two can catch this guy before he kills someone else. The press will soon dub him a serial killer. One more murder and they'll have a field day."

When they left Fillmore's office, they got in the car and headed for the home of Willard Jakes, father of Garner Jakes.

"I don't expect to learn much from the old man," Davis said, "but we need to uncover the cause of the rift between him and his son. It might give us a clue to Garner's motivations."

"It might also give us a clue to who had it in for him, who might have wanted him dead."

They found Willard Jakes to be talkative, opinionated, and clearly disgusted with his son for having gotten himself murdered. He needed little urging to get him to talk about his son's character, particularly his failings.

"From the day we got him," Willard declared, "Garner was contrary and stubborn. A self-centered, opinionated boy, who would listen to no one, especially his parents."

"Are you telling us Garner was adopted?"

"My wife Ellie had a hysterectomy early in our marriage. She insisted on adopting a child. I opposed the adoption but gave in when I saw how much it meant to her. She had the notion an adopted child would be filled with gratitude for our having given him a home. Garner became resentful instead. Because we were not his real parents, we had no right, in his view, to discipline him or make decisions for his future. We settled into an atmosphere of controlled hostility."

"Most children go through a rebellious stage as they grow up," Fulford said. "But they get over it with the passage of time. Didn't Garner's attitude ever show signs of change?"

"It took a tragedy to affect him. After a long remission of the cancer that had forced her to have a hysterectomy, Ellie had a recurrence. The doctor told her she had only a month or two to live. Garner began to treat her with civility at first, and finally with tenderness. Our relationship, his and mine, improved, too. I began to hope Garner and I might become close.

"When Ellie finally died, Garner stood by her coffin, the very picture of grief. He cried. He stood there a long time, looking at her body from every vantage point. He seemed in the grip of some morbid fascination. After the funeral, he came to me and said, 'Mom's death has shown me what I want to do with my life. I hope you will approve.' I assumed his mother's death had moved him to enter one of the helping professions. I hoped he was going to tell me he wanted to become a doctor.

"I told him that medicine was a noble profession, one I would be proud for him to pursue. I told him I would be happy to pay his expenses at one of the best medical schools in the country.

"He smiled in an odd way and said, 'I hadn't been thinking of medical school, Dad. I want to become an undertaker.' "

"Were you terribly disappointed?" asked Davis.

"I argued with him until I was blue in the face. I pointed out that, in terms of prestige, financial gain, and contribution to the public welfare, undertaking was an inferior trade. Why not, I asked him, devote your life to keeping people alive rather than consigning them to the grave? Nothing swayed him. When he graduated from junior college, he went to a mortician's school here in Atlanta. He's been practicing, if that's the word, for a little over a year. And not very successfully, I might add."

"I sense his decision caused a serious rift between you."

"I'll never forgive him. He'd be alive today if he hadn't gone into that business."

"Why do you say that?" asked Fulford.

"Well, he got murdered by another undertaker, didn't he?"

"That hasn't been established," Davis said, "but it's a possibility. I'm curious why you say that. Did he have enemies among his colleagues?"

"I'm sure he did. He told me he had stumbled upon serious unethical behavior by a man he knew. Perhaps criminal behavior. He was greatly disturbed about it and uncertain what to do."

"Did he tell you the man was an undertaker?"

"Not in so many words. But given the circumstances, I thought that's what he meant."

"I assume he didn't tell you who the man was and what he had done?"

"No, he didn't. I wish now he had. I wish I had insisted on him telling me. It would help you apprehend his murderer. I was surprised he told me as much as he did. He was not in the habit of confiding in me."

Willard Jakes's bitterness toward his son was evident in every inflection of his voice. Fulford felt there must have been some other reason for his ill will, beyond his son's defiance in becoming a mortician. She disliked the man and decided to press him a bit.

"Your son was adopted. You've already told us he was ungrateful toward you and your wife. Was it your belief he behaved the way he did because he wasn't of your own flesh and blood?"

Jakes answered the question without taking offense. His reply was given in a judicial tone, as if he had given the matter much thought and had come to a carefully considered conclusion.

"Adoption is a gamble. People suppose they can train a child, regardless of heredity, in the way they want him or her to go. Sometimes they can. Sometimes they fail."

He paused. Before he could continue, Fulford intervened.

"In Garner's case, do you think you failed because he was of inferior stock?"

"I'd say that's evident, wouldn't you?"

The next day they were sitting in Davis's office, sipping an early morning coffee, and reflecting on Willard Jakes's comments about his son, especially his belief that Garner had discovered unethical behavior on the part of one of his colleagues. "If his father is right," Davis said, "then we have a possible motive for Garner's murder. Garner must have told the person he suspected of unethical behavior what he knew, and the person felt obliged to silence him."

Fulford frowned. "He must have done something serious to warrant murdering Garner. Was it something that might have gotten the person disbarred from his profession or opened him up to serious sanctions from his colleagues if it became known? Or worse, could it have been criminal behavior?"

"The latter, most likely," Davis said. "Few people would be willing to commit murder except when faced with some extraordinary risk. Like the prospect of a long term in prison."

"I suppose there's an association of undertakers in the city. If we make some inquiries there, we can probably find out who he was friendly with. The person who murdered him would have to be someone who knew him reasonably well. I'll see what I can find later this morning."

They fell silent. Fulford felt the tension between them and knew the reason for it. Since their date, and the intimacy it brought, Davis's behavior toward her had undergone a subtle change. He had, unobtrusively at first, but with growing openness, acted toward her as if, by her recent impulsive surrender, she had committed herself to a lasting relationship. She was unsure of her feelings toward him and kept backing away. He was, she admitted, an uncommonly attractive man, a man who had many of the attributes of an ideal mate, but she was unwilling at this point to tie herself to him, or to any other man.

Davis had been covertly watching her and, sensing her ambivalence toward him, asked, "Leda, are you dating Chris McCalmon?"

The question startled her. She wondered if Davis actually knew about the date or if he were simply guessing. Perhaps, and this was a disturbing thought, McCalmon had bragged to Davis about it in a spirit of friendly rivalry. Either way, the question was intrusive, and it irked her.

"What if I have, Wade? Am I supposed to account to you for the men I date?"

"Of course not. I just thought we were close enough to share things of that nature. After all, we're not exactly strangers."

"No, we're not. Neither are we married or engaged."

"I thought something like that might be in our future."

Fulford was unprepared for this near proposal. "Wade, I think you've made too much of the evening I spent with you. What I did was the result of a momentary impulse. I certainly don't regret it, but I don't want you to make more of it than you should. I wish I had followed my mama's advice. It would have been better for both of us if I had."

She paused, keeping her eyes on Davis. When she spoke again, she intended to be honest and forthright. "Yes, I had a date with Chris two nights ago. We went to a cat show at the Civic Center."

Davis said impulsively, "I suppose you slept with him, too."

Fulford flushed but kept her anger in check. "That's a nasty thing to say, Wade. Maybe someday I can forgive you."

Further angry words, on the tip of her tongue, were not said because Albert Saffron appeared at the office door, flourishing a copy of the morning newspaper, which he waved in their faces as if it held news of an armistice in a long war.

"I can tell neither of you have read the morning paper," he said. "Your hangdog manner, your lack of enthusiasm, your dampened spirits tell me you've made absolutely no progress in solving the case of the nefarious necrophiliac, or the butcher bird, or whatever . . . But take heart. Let me read you an article I discovered as I downed my morning coffee. I will then propound a theory, a theory so compelling, your spirits will soar at the expectation of victory over the forces of evil."

"After that bombastic hype, you'd better have something good," Davis said.

Albert smirked. "Believe me. I have. Listen to this."

JUDGE ORDERS EXHUMATION

> After several months of heated argument, a bitter legal wrangle over the exhumation of the body of a local man's wife has been resolved by Judge Farleigh Tremont. Tremont has ordered the exhumation, tomorrow morning, of the body of Julia Wills, so that her remains may be tested for poison.
>
> "Since the beginning of our romance," Herbert Wills, the husband, contended, "Julia's parents have sought to discredit me. They accused me of marrying Julia for her money and tried in every way they could to persuade her to divorce me. She refused to be swayed by them and stayed loyal to me."
>
> John Mayhew, Julia's father, accuses his son-in-law of murdering his daughter with some kind of unknown poison. He believes the residue of such a substance may still be present in her tissues. His daughter died suddenly, he points out, and Herbert Wills's refusal to allow an autopsy for alleged religious reasons—he maintains he is a devout Christian Scientist—is a justifiable cause for suspicion.

"There's more," Albert said. "It seems Julia Wills was left some property, about two hundred acres in California, near Los Angeles, by an uncle who was killed in a plane crash. An immense deposit of oil was recently discovered beneath her land, making her a potential millionaire.

"About this time, she met Herbert Wills, and the two fell in love. When he proposed marriage, Julia's parents had a fit. Herbert Wills was a man of modest prospects. He was a salesperson at the time, an associate in the electronics division of a local department store. In spite of her parents' objections, they were married. Six months later, Julia died of a respiratory disease, a mysterious ailment which behaved like emphysema. On the death certificate, the doctor listed acute bronchitis and edema.

"The parents demanded an autopsy, but Herbert's objections on religious grounds prevailed. She was buried, but her parents began a long legal battle to have her body exhumed and examined for several poisons. They finally convinced Judge Tremont to order the exhumation when they were able to establish that Herbert Wills had inquired of a friend, shortly before Julia's death, how to extract atropine from belladonna plants."

He paused, looking at the detectives with anticipation.

Davis appeared puzzled, a quizzical expression on his face. "I'm not sure I see your point, Albert," he said. "Do you think Herbert Wills murdered his wife? If so, what would that have to do with the murder of Donovan Grey and Garner Jakes?"

Albert's manner was that of a profound thinker instructing his duller colleagues. "I don't know if Herbert Wills murdered his wife. If he did, I'm sure he had nothing to do with any other murders. What Wills did or did not do to Julia is irrelevant. What's important is this: The body of the young woman you found at Proctor Creek is, I believe, that of Julia Wills. Why do I think that? Our necrophiliac abducts Julia's body, before or after her funeral, and keeps her stashed away for his sexual pleasure.

"Then he reads about the attempt to exhume her body. When it becomes apparent Judge Tremont is likely to order her dug up, he panics. If her grave is opened, the theft of her body will be revealed, and suspicion will fall upon him for a very valid reason. Because," he paused for dramatic effect, "he was the undertaker who buried her."

Fulford objected, "Why should her undertaker be suspected over some unknown person? Anyone could have dug up her grave and stolen her body."

"Not if I'm right about what happened," Albert said. "If you're too dull to figure it out, I refuse to tell you what the guy did. Join me at the exhumation tomorrow morning. Things will become clear."

"You can be sure we'll be there," Davis said, "but there's no reason in the world for you to go. You're not assigned to the case."

"Makes no difference," Albert replied. "I've an imperative reason for attending. I've never seen a funeral in reverse. I wouldn't miss it."

"There *is* somebody who really ought be there," Fulford said. "Gerry Fillmore. Hadn't we better clue him in on this?"

Davis got on the phone. "Gerry?" he said. "The body of a woman named Julia Wills is to be exhumed tomorrow morning. I thought I'd better let you know in case you're interested."

"Judge Tremont has already contacted me," Fillmore replied.

"Mrs. Wills's body is being exhumed to determine if a homicide by poisoning has been committed. Who else would he ask to make that determination but our forensics people? I assume you and Fulford are going."

After listening to Fillmore repeat what Judge Tremont had told him, Davis hung up the phone. "Homicide Division will be well represented at tomorrow morning's shindig. Expect a crowd. You'll be pleased to know, Albert, if you insist on indulging your morbid curiosity, you'll have to pay a price. The grave diggers begin their work at five."

Chapter Eleven

The cemetery at that predawn hour had a ghostly aura, created by wisps of fog that wandered among the tombstones like resurrected souls. As Davis and his companions approached, two shafts of light from portable mercury vapor lamps swept the ground and settled upon a stone bearing the legend, JULIA WILLS 1966–1986. Beside the grave stood an old couple, holding hands, staring somberly at the stone. Julia's parents. Opposite them was a young man, face set in harsh, angry lines, staring malevolently at the older couple.

A police officer motioned the three away from the grave, and, without a word being said, a backhoe coughed to life, and the operator began gouging scoops of earth from the grave and piling them to one side. In a short time, he had delved about four feet below the surface, at which point he backed his machine away, and two men with shovels continued the digging. In about fifteen minutes, the coffin was exposed, straps were wormed beneath it, and the coffin itself was raised to the surface and lifted to one side.

Judge Tremont stepped into the circle of bright light that surrounded the palely gleaming mahogany box. In solemn tones, he said, "The lid of this coffin is about to be removed in compliance with the orders of the court. Should anyone not wish to be present for this deed, they may be excused."

He paused, looking pointedly at Julia Wills's parents and then her husband.

No one moved.

"Very well," the judge said, nodding to the two men who were, Davis surmised, employees of the mortuary. "You may proceed."

They quickly unfastened the lid, lifted it, and set it aside.

All present pressed forward and gaped into the coffin. Consternation, disbelief, and astonishment showed on every face, for the coffin held no human form. Instead, lying end to end on the plush bed of the casket were two fifty-pound bags of fertilizer.

Albert Saffron looked at Fulford and Davis.

"I guessed it," he whispered triumphantly. "I don't have to tell you where Julia Wills's body is. She's been in our custody for days."

Fulford gave Davis a knowing glance that said, "I once guessed at something like this. Why are we so surprised?"

Julia Wills's parents broke into tears. Arms around each other, eyes red and cheeks wet, they glared hatefully at Herbert Wills. Wills looked stunned, totally unnerved. His chin trembled spasmodically, and he looked around as if searching for a sympathetic face.

As the detectives watched, Farleigh Tremont walked up to Wills and said something. Wills nodded, turned around, walked to his car, got in, and drove away.

John Mayhew and his wife protested to Tremont, speaking heatedly, expressions insolent, gestures fierce. Tremont listened calmly, answered firmly, then turned away and consulted with the workmen. Having given them orders, he also got in his car and drove away.

Fillmore eyed Davis, Fulford, and Saffron with some disgust. "There isn't much doubt about the identity of the girl we have in our cooler, is there? We'll have to have Herbert Wills look at her. I think, however, we'd better give him time to get over his shock."

Herbert Wills obeyed the summons and appeared at the M.E.'s office at precisely three o'clock. Awaiting the arrival of the detectives, he sat bent forward, as if a heavy weight were bearing down on his shoulders. A small man, he had the air of a person who had suffered a severe physical blow and was wracked with pain. When she saw him, Fulford characterized him as being deeply depressed but seething with anger.

Wills got up without speaking when the detectives entered and merely nodded as they introduced themselves. He seemed to have little interest in the proceedings. Davis said, "We have the body of a woman in our possession who we think may be your wife. We would like you to look at her, and if she is indeed Mrs. Wills, we will want to talk with you at length."

Davis's statement shook Wills out of his lethargy. He stood up, paced nervously for a few moments, then sat, drumming on the chair arm with fingers that appeared to be fluttering out of control.

"I cannot imagine she's my wife," he said, shaking his head. "But then I cannot imagine why my wife was not in her coffin. What could have happened to her?"

"Perhaps we can tell you what happened," Davis said, "after you've looked at the body."

He took Wills by the arm and guided him into the morgue, where Christopher McCalmon pulled open a drawer and lifted the sheet from the corpse's face, being careful not to expose the mutilated shoulder and arm. Wills looked briefly, then turned aside. His face was twisted with pain, and he began to cry.

Fulford rested a hand on his shoulder and said sympathetically, "We're sorry, but there was no way we could cushion the shock. Why don't you come back with us to Detective Davis's office for a cup of coffee?"

She handed him a small packet of tissues, and he followed her out the door. Davis walked behind them.

"We believe," Davis said, when they reached his office, "that someone removed your wife's body before her funeral. At the ceremony, the coffin was buried without her, empty except for the bags of fertilizer."

Wills sipped his coffee and said with great self control, "I suppose you're right. If Julia's body had been removed after she was buried, there would have been no point in putting the bags of fertilizer in her coffin. The fertilizer was necessary to make the coffin appear heavy enough to contain her body. But who could have done such a thing?"

"We were inclined to suspect your undertaker," Davis said. "An undertaker could easily have carried out the theft with little prospect of being caught."

"But Garner Jakes was the undertaker. He's an honorable man. What motive could he have had for doing a thing like that? What would he gain from stealing Julia's body?"

"Although we suspected Jakes," Davis said, "events have shown he could not have been the culprit. You see, Jakes was murdered last night."

Wills heard the news with a puzzled expression on his face. "If Jakes didn't do it, who did? I suppose you have other suspects?"

Davis uttered one of his obligatory lies, "Yes, but I am not at liberty to disclose their names. Thanks for your help, Mr. Wills. We'll keep in touch."

They dismissed him abruptly. He left the office baffled, bereaved, and disconsolate.

"He's in a mess," Fulford observed. "Not only must he confront the fact that his wife's body has been stolen, but he has to surrender it on the judge's order for forensics to play with. And then he must face a potential murder charge leveled by his in-laws."

"I agree he's got plenty of troubles. I hope he doesn't come unhinged. But we've got problems, too, Leda. Someone removed Julia's body from the casket and left two bags of fertilizer in her place. It wasn't Jakes. So, dear Leda, who done it? Any ideas?"

Fulford inspected her fingernails thoughtfully. "Her undertaker was the obvious suspect, but he was killed."

"So someone other than Jakes had to do it. Agreed?"

"Not necessarily," Fulford said. "Think of it this way. Garner Jakes became an undertaker because of an unnatural attraction to the dead. He's a true necrophiliac. I think his father suspected there was some odd kind of motivation for his choice to become an undertaker. Remember what he said about Garner's fascination with his mother's dead body. Let's assume Garner struggled with his obsession and never gave in to it until he received a commission to bury Julia Wills, an uncommonly beautiful young woman. He falls in love with her body and makes plans to steal her and keep her for his own twisted desires. After the casket is closed for the last time, but before the procession to the cemetery takes place, he secretly removes her and puts the fertilizer bags in her place.

"If Garner didn't do it, who else had the opportunity? The fact he was murdered doesn't mean he couldn't have done it."

"Wait," Davis said. "I remind you again, we agreed Donovan Grey and Garner Jakes were killed by the same person. The evidence supported that assumption then, and it still does. Look at the consequences of your reasoning. Do you now believe we have two killers?"

"Yes, I do. Jakes killed Donovan Grey because Grey saw him dump Julia's body and throw her severed arm into Proctor Creek. Willard Jakes told us his son had discovered unethical, possibly criminal behavior on the part of one of his colleagues, probably another undertaker. We don't know who that person was or what he had done, but when Garner confronted him with the knowledge he had, the guy murdered him."

Davis smiled at Fulford in a patronizing way. "I give you credit, Leda, for an elegant theory. Unfortunately, there's not a shred of evidence to support it."

Fulford shook her head ruefully and laughed. "It makes up for the lack of evidence by its elegance. You have to admit it ties up all the strings very neatly."

"Okay, it's neat. But I've got a neat theory of my own. How about this? Jakes was taking lessons in how to make leaded glass from Ralph Hamlet. If we believe, as we have all along, that the person who threw Julia's arm into the Chattahoochee had access to a supply of came, then Ralph Hamlet becomes a suspect. I'm going to assume, for the moment, that Hamlet is our culprit. He certainly had his hands on all the came he wanted.

"Let's assume also—I seem to be making as many assumptions as you did—that in the course of his visits to Hamlet's bomb-shelter workshop, Jakes stumbles upon the fact that Hamlet has the body of a woman hidden in the storage space Weldon Knowles told us about.

"Jakes is not a necrophiliac, as you have assumed. In fact, he's outraged at what he has discovered and confronts Hamlet. Hamlet pretends to be contrite and promises to put Julia's body back in her grave. But he doesn't. He takes her to Proctor Creek where, after raping her, he abandons her. He is seen by Donovan Grey. Whether Donovan saw the actual rape, we don't know, but Hamlet knows he is a serious threat and lays plans to dispose of him. Jakes reads the paper, guesses what is going on, and calls us, promising to identify the body; but before he does, he wants to talk to Hamlet. Maybe he wants to give him a chance to flee. Maybe he has something else in mind, like blackmail. We don't know. He invites Hamlet to his home, and Hamlet comes prepared to silence him, just as he silenced Donnie Grey."

He paused, awaiting Fulford's reaction.

"I suppose," she said, "both your theory and mine have some elements of truth in them. The crucial difference is that your theory puts a lot of reliance on the murderer being someone with access to came. I don't think that's a critical factor. Garner bought came during his lessons with Hamlet, but his possession of it is immaterial. My theory is based on the fact that Jakes is far more likely to be a necrophiliac, given his history, than Hamlet. And he had greater opportunity to get his hands on a body. In fact, I don't see how Hamlet could have, in any likely way, gotten hold of Mrs. Wills's body."

Davis was not inclined to further argue the merits of the two theories. Neither seemed, at the moment, to have anything to substantiate them. The guesswork they had indulged in, however, had at least one advantage. It pointed to two possible suspects: Ralph Hamlet, and an unknown acquaintance of Jake, who, threatened by Jakes's discovery of derogatory information about him, had a reason to do away with him.

"I'll tell you what I think we ought to do," he said. "You begin trying to link Jakes with a friend or colleague who might have had reason to kill him, and I'll see if I can unearth something on Ralph Hamlet. I'm thinking of enlisting the help of Kim Kendall. Get her to approach Hamlet, pretending to be interested in learning how to make stained glass objects."

"Do you think it wise to involve her? Didn't Knowles say she tried her best to seduce Hamlet?"

"And Kim told me it was the other way around. Who knows what the truth is. Either way, Kim ought to be able to get a look at what's in Hamlet's workshop."

He changed the subject abruptly in response to a nagging sense of unease about the strained relationship between Fulford and him. No other woman since the death of his wife had appealed to him so strongly. The intimacy that had occurred the night of their first date had swept through his emotions with such a firestorm, he could not think of losing her to another man without a sense of utter panic.

"How was your date with Chris?" he asked with elaborate unconcern.

Fulford was not deceived. In a way she was pleased at his evident jealousy. Knowing that deep down her affection for Davis was growing, she said, "I didn't sleep with him, if that's what you want to know."

He looked at her in surprise. He had not expected such directness and wondered how to respond. He could be honest and tell her how incredibly happy he was at the news, or he could pretend it was a matter of indifference. He found the latter impossible.

"I'm glad," he said, "although I would not have been surprised if you had. Chris is a very attractive man."

"He is that. We went to a cat show. Cat Fanciers of America, or some such organization. I learned more about cats," she said with an inward smile, "than I ever thought I wanted to know."

She paused. Then, with a mischievous smile, she said, "Did you know female cats have a bifurcated uterus?"

"No, I didn't, but it's the kind of information Chris stores away to astonish people with. Did he bore you?"

"No, he didn't. He was charming."

Davis grinned. "I can be charming, too. Maybe I even hold an edge over Chris in that department. In fact, I'm so convinced of it, I'm tempted to ask you for another date. Will you go with me to see a performance of the ballet *Giselle*?"

She pretended to give the invitation a great deal of solemn thought, then said with refreshing eagerness, "I'd be glad to. The only classical ballet I've seen is *Sleeping Beauty*. I was brought up on modern dance."

"Well, nothing, in my opinion, can equal classical ballet. When you see *Giselle*, I'm sure you'll agree with me."

"Don't be too sure. I wasn't exactly knocked out of my senses by *Sleeping Beauty*. Tell me, Wade, when's the performance?"

"Tonight at eight."

"Tonight! I can't believe I'm hearing you right. You're asking me at eleven o'clock in the morning to attend a performance at eight the same day?"

"I admit it's short notice. You don't have a date with someone else, do you?"

He was reluctant to tell her he had bought the tickets days before and was afraid, until the last moment, to ask her to go.

"No, I don't. But I'm tempted to back out just to teach you a lesson in manners."

"Please don't do that, Leda. Next time, I'll ask you weeks in advance."

She had no real reason to be upset. She had no plans for the evening. There would be no difficulty getting dressed after work. Still, she had a sense of exasperation.

"What would you have done if I had said no?"

"Cried. That's what."

In spite of herself, Fulford had to laugh.

Giselle, with the Georgia Ballet and the Atlanta Symphony, was performed in the Civic Center. The building lacked the imposing aura of the Woodruff Arts Center, but it had its own kind of charm, and the crowd, unlike the fashionably garbed audience they had seen at the Alliance, was subdued in dress and manner. Fulford, clued in by Davis, wore a simple skirt and blouse with a pale blue cardigan draped about her shoulders. Davis had on a business suit.

When the curtain rose on the dazzling set—Giselle's cottage in the left foreground, the woods in the background, the hunter's cabin to the right—Fulford was fascinated. She was totally entranced as the music swelled and the strikingly costumed dancers began to move.

She followed the story with ease. Giselle, a marvelous dancer, has a weak heart and is prohibited from dancing because of it. But two men, one the aristocrat Albrecht, the other the commoner Hilarion, woo her, and in spite of her ailment, she is provoked into dancing for Albrecht. She fancies Albrecht so much, she dances for him with reckless abandon. She dies from the exertion and must join the Wilis, a ghostly troop composed of the spirits of young, betrothed women who died before they could marry.

During the only intermission, she said to Davis, "I've often heard people say that something gave them the wilis. I always thought wilis was spelled w-i-l-l-i-e-s, and I never could understand why willies could be threatening."

"Wilis have existed in folklore for ages," Davis said. "They were threatening because, if a living person sought to follow and speak to them, that person would be forced to dance with them 'til he or she died of exhaustion. Giselle became one of the Wilis because she disobeyed her mother's instructions to limit her dancing and died from her exertions."

"I hope the second act is as good as the first," Fulford said.

"You'll love it," Davis predicted. "You'll see what happens to Albrecht and Hilarion as they pursue Giselle beyond the grave."

She loved it, indeed, and was eager to tell Davis how delightful and intriguing she found it. When Davis invited her to have a nightcap at his apartment, she accepted without reflection.

"I see a connection between the story of *Giselle* and the case we're investigating," she said as she settled down with a drink. "Both Albrecht and Hilarion are so in love with Giselle, they refuse to give her up, even though she's dead. They follow her beyond the grave, despite the risk of being captured by the Wilis and forced to dance until, completely exhausted, they die."

"Do you think Albrecht and Hilarion are like the person who abducted Julia Wills's body?"

"I do. *Giselle* is about two men trying to hold on to the love they had for a woman by, in a sense, visiting her in the grave. This is the way I see it. Julia Wills, beloved wife of Herbert Wills, dies, not from poison as her parents think, but because of an acute respiratory infection as her husband contends. Herbert is out of his mind with grief, and like Albrecht, pursues his lover beyond the grave. But his is not a romantic trip to the land of the Wilis. He simply removes her body from the coffin and replaces it with bags of fertilizer. He hides her away where he can dote upon her at leisure."

"I'm impressed with your ingenuity, Leda," Davis said. "And your analogy is really striking. You're thinking of Herbert Wills as the personification of Albrecht. But what about Hilarion? We can have another person who loved Julia as much as her husband did. He could be the one who stole Julia's body."

"Yes, but why conjure up another suspect when the husband is the obvious one?"

"Well, we're dealing in mythology, aren't we? Why limit ourselves to anything?"

He paused, a smile of amusement on his face. "You're really good at seeing improbable likenesses, Leda. I never would have thought of necrophilia in connection with one of the world's most renowned romantic ballets. But I have to admit, there's a curious kind of logic to it."

"You're too literal minded, that's all."

"You're probably right. But let's get back to the affairs of the living. Are you going to spend the night with me?"

She looked at him with a strange expression, one that had in it signs of real affection, but also signs of an odd remoteness and a disconcerting ambivalence.

"Not tonight," she said. "Maybe another time. Will you take me home, Wade?"

Chapter Twelve

The whole scheme had an element of conspiracy about it, perhaps even entrapment, but he justified himself with the age-old argument that a good end excuses dubious means. He took Fulford with him when he set out to recruit Kim Kendall, cautioning her to remain silent unless he asked her to speak. "Your role," he said, "is to provide same-sex assurance to a young woman who may get the idea she is being manipulated by a male for undisclosed purposes."

"Isn't that exactly what you're doing, Wade? Why should I help you bamboozle an innocent young girl?"

"I'm not bamboozling her. I'm merely going to ask her, as a good citizen, to cooperate with the police." To this he added what seemed to him an invincible argument, "We're dealing with murder here, Leda. What else can we do?"

"Why not drop a project that has nothing going for it except your conviction that Hamlet is a necrophiliac?"

She paused, but seeing the stubborn expression on his face, she said, "All right, I'll play along on the possibility you might be right about Hamlet."

Kim, apparently eager to please, and even more eager to see herself in the role of undercover sleuth, readily consented to Davis's request.

"All you need do," Davis said, "is pretend you are interested in learning to work with stained glass. Get Professor Hamlet to give you instruction in his bomb-shelter studio. You shouldn't find that difficult. You told me he showed an interest in you one time when you stayed after class. You should be able to reawaken that interest."

"Suppose I do?" Kim asked. "What am I to look for? You're interested in uncovering something in the bomb shelter, aren't you?"

"We are," Davis admitted, "but we can't tell you exactly what.

Just look for anything out of the ordinary, anything that doesn't seem to fit with the requirements of a glass studio. Also, we'd like a detailed description of the layout of the place."

Kim reflected on Davis's vague directive.

"I'm not so dumb," she said with a trace of impertinence. "I'll bet this has something to do with the murder of Garner Jakes. I read he had been taking instruction in glassmaking from Professor Hamlet. Do you think the professor murdered Jakes?"

"Kim, please keep the lid on your curiosity. Just get in there and let us know what you find. Okay?"

"Ten-four. I'll be looking for a smoking gun. When do I start?"

After Kim had gone, Fulford looked at Davis and smiled.

"How did you like the ten-four, Wade?"

Davis returned her smile. "And the smoking gun. I think we have an eager, very obliging recruit."

In the hope of locating professional friends or acquaintances of Garner Jakes, Fulford asked for an appointment with Baxter Cawthon, president of Cawthon's School of Burial Science, the institution from which Jakes had graduated.

Effusive as he had been when the detectives had visited him initially, Cawthon seemed to outdo himself in buttering up Fulford. As he ushered her into his office, he said, "My dear Ms. Fulford. Would you like some coffee, some Coke, a drink, perhaps?"

Although she found him distasteful for some indefinable reason, Fulford responded to his studied affability.

"Thank you. Coffee would be fine," she said. "Black."

He buzzed a secretary, and the coffee appeared quickly. Fulford noted with interest that the secretary was one of Cawthon's students. She also noted the tasteful appointments of the office. She was seated on a sofa that, judging from the rich fabric that covered it, had come from one of Atlanta's plusher furniture stores. So, too, the desk behind which Cawthon sat. It was made of a rich, lustrous wood, pecan or something similar, and its luster, she was sure, came from repeated hand rubbing. On the tastefully papered walls hung framed diplomas, certificates of advanced study, and letters attesting to the gratitude and adulation of former students. Cawthon, it appeared, was a highly successful man.

"You have read, no doubt, of the murder of Garner Jakes," she said as she sipped her coffee.

Cawthon's expression was one of great sorrow, as if he had experienced a personal bereavement.

"Such a fine, upstanding member of our profession. His is a great loss. Have you apprehended the murderer?"

"Unfortunately not. We are still in the preliminary stages of the investigation. That's why I have come to you."

"You may be assured I will assist the police in any way I can."

Again Fulford had the impression of forced geniality.

"He graduated from your school, did he not?"

"Something over eighteen months ago. He was a very apt student." Cawthon's face assumed a remote expression, as if he were lost in recollection. "Very few students have the kind of genuine devotion to the profession young Jakes had. The meticulous care he lavished on a body was something to be admired. And I admired him for it."

"So you and he were more than teacher and student, I take it. You were friends?"

"He wanted to practice here in Atlanta. I helped him get established. Gave him a hand now and then, when he needed it. I'd say I was more a mentor than a friend. We didn't see each other socially."

"Did he have friends among your other students?"

"There was a woman from Marietta, a Gwendolyn Smith, in whom he showed some interest. Incidentally, there are very few women in the profession. Doesn't seem to suit them. I think she and Garner had several dates. She's practicing in Marietta, I believe."

"Did he make any enemies you know of?"

"He was, as I have told you, very meticulous, very exacting in his work. Some of the other students found him irritating. He would criticize their work, particularly in the art of cosmetic restoration. I'm sure I told you on your first visit that morticians need to rebuild the features of a corpse that had been disfigured by disease or accident. Jakes was very good at this and intolerant of sloppy work on the part of others."

"Hardly a cause for serious enmity, I'd say. Can you think of any conflict of consequence between him and others? Anything that might have prompted murder?"

"I doubt if this incident could have prompted murder, but it did lead to ill will between Jakes and a student with the improbable name Hercules Brown. Brown claimed he had seen Jakes fondling a female body, the body of a very young and attractive girl. The alleged incident occurred after work was over for the day and as Brown was leaving the lab. He saw Jakes doing something to the body. Jakes did not deny he was with the body. He *did* deny he was fondling it. Said he was rubbing it with skin cream to stop the dryness that was beginning to set in."

"Whom did you believe?"

"Hercules Brown was a misfit. Nobody liked him, and in a few days he dropped out of school. I believed Garner. What he did would have been consistent with his insistence on quality care for our clientele. And anyway, if the incident was the cause of violence, I should think Garner was the aggrieved party. He would have taken revenge on Brown. If Brown indeed felt resentment against Jakes for some imaginary reason, why would he wait until now to do him in?"

"Good point. Do you have any idea where Hercules Brown is living?"

"None. I know he was from Alabama. I suppose he went back there."

Fulford, recognizing the Hercules Brown affair was probably a dead end, raised a question she thought might bring more fruitful results. "You said you helped Jakes get established in business and gave him a hand now and then. When you say 'gave him a hand,' what sort of things do you mean?"

"Well, I helped him embalm his first few clients. He and his assistant—he had only one—lacked confidence at first. They were happy to have me supervise. I also coached him on how to appeal to a family's wish to give their loved one a suitable burial."

Fulford interpreted this remark to mean Cawthon had coached his student in the art of selling expensive caskets, and the propriety of hiring limousines for the funeral procession. She suppressed the impulse to make a sarcastic remark.

"His assistant at the time of his murder was Richard Cheatham. Is he the same one you worked with when you assisted Jakes with his first clients?"

"He's the man."

Fulford saw nothing more to be gained from Cawthon. She had the distinct impression he disclosed only what suited him and withheld information that could have been important to her case. Perhaps, if he knew additional facts, she could force him to be more forthcoming at a future time.

Had the story of Hercules Brown been given her to plant the notion that Jakes might be unnaturally interested in female corpses? She did not, at the moment, see what purpose Cawthon could have had in making such a ploy. He could not have been aware of her hypothesis, argued so heatedly with Davis, that Jakes was a necrophiliac.

Kim had no trouble getting Hamlet to show her how to make leaded glass. In fact, he seemed eager to oblige her. Kim, who was bold in spirit, saw no threat in working alone with him in the isolation of the bomb shelter. She sensed he found her attractive from the way he looked at her when he thought she didn't notice. His glance, while frankly appreciative, had a strange element to it. There was an element of discovery, as if he recognized some archetypal image hidden beneath her face and form. Yet he made no overtures. He never touched her, never spoke a suggestive word.

He began by showing her how easy it is to cut glass in a straight line. As a first project, she made a rectangle containing an abstract design that required only straight cuts. He showed her how to assemble the pieces into the channels of the came, hold the pattern together with nails, and solder the joints.

She became so engrossed in the task, she almost forgot her duty as a sleuth. At first, she had little opportunity to find out what the rest of the bomb shelter was like. Hamlet was at her side constantly, and she could find no excuse to go wandering about the premises.

As she grew more at ease, she told Hamlet she had to use the bathroom. He showed her where it was and returned to the studio. Complaining of a bladder problem, she visited the toilet often. Each time, she was able to catch brief glimpses of other parts of the shelter. There appeared to be just two spaces other than the studio—a small kitchenette, and a pantry-like cavity that appeared to have been dug into the rear wall as an afterthought. In this space, which was about eight feet wide, but vertically only about the height of Kim's shoulders, a cabinet had been built. It had two doors that split its surface horizontally. Hinged at the top and bottom, the two doors met in the center, where they were secured with a hasp and a padlock.

Probably a place for storing food, Kim thought, but then realized the cabinet, from the newness of its appearance, had been installed recently. Probably no more than a year ago or thereabouts. It was not for storing came or glass; those items were arranged in racks along the walls of the studio. Food and beverages, in small quantities, were kept on shelves in the kitchenette. She wondered what was inside the rather mysterious cabinet. She would ask Davis, her attractive mentor, what magical device from his store of spy equipment she could use to discover its contents.

Her first session with Hamlet ended at four o'clock. He escorted her to her car and said, "I hope you found your session with me enjoyable. You are an apt student, and I predict you will quickly be producing sophisticated glass artifacts. Shall we have another session tomorrow?"

"Thank you," Kim replied. "I'll be seeing you."

She went straight to the police station and reported to Detective Davis.

When she explained the problem of the cabinet to him, he gave her a wide-bladed screwdriver and instructed her on how to insert it between the doors and pry in hope of creating a gap large enough to see through. In addition, given the probability the interior of the cabinet would be dark, he gave her a pencil-thin flashlight.

When he saw the look of disappointment fall across her face, he said, "Often simple devices, Kim, are better than more sophisticated ones. And these you can carry in your purse."

Kim nodded in compliance and put the implements in her purse. "I was hoping you had some sort of portable x-ray device," she said. "That would have been fun."

"We use that kind of equipment," Davis said, "only as a last resort. I trust you to make good use of the screwdriver."

Kim promised to do her best and prepared for her final and most terrifying lesson in the art of making stained glass.

Before she left, Davis asked if she had noticed anything odd, even a minor detail about Hamlet's studio. She was about to shake her head in the negative, then, remembering, she volunteered one thing.

"The refrigerator seems to run a lot. You would think, because it's below ground, it would run less than normal. But it doesn't. It puzzled me a bit."

"Are you sure it isn't the air conditioner you hear?"

"It could be. I'll check it out tomorrow when I go back."

As she and Ralph Hamlet descended into the bomb shelter for her second lesson, Kim became aware that her instructor had more on his mind than cutting glass and soldering came. At first he glanced furtively at her, then more directly and, in her opinion, more lecherously.

He made her nervous, but not truly afraid. She had learned, from dating eager college men, several ways of turning off sexual overtures. Although this situation was different, in that she was sequestered in an isolated spot with a potential attacker, she trusted her ability to cope with any approach Hamlet might make. Hamlet, who on her previous visit had said little except to offer explanations and instructions, now suddenly said, "Kim, have you ever given any thought to what produces interpersonal attraction?"

"I'm not sure I know what you mean, Professor Hamlet," Kim replied. She placed an ever so slight emphasis on the words "Professor Hamlet" in order to remind him of his professional status, his role in a student-teacher relationship.

He put his hand over hers as it rested on the table.

"I mean, why is it we sometimes select one person out of a multitude and then, as Emily Dickinson wrote, 'close the valves of out attention like stone'?"

Kim withdrew her hand and gave him a reproachful look. "Professor Hamlet, I hope you aren't going to put the make on me. You're nice, and I like you. I'd be happy to be your friend. But that's it. No cozy little intimacies or anything like that."

Hamlet seemed slightly taken aback but persisted. "Don't be in a hurry to reject something that may be to your advantage, Kim. I could do a lot for you. I could help you with your academic career, and I would bring you love and devotion. Only once before in my life have I been so attracted to a woman. I wonder what it is about you that draws me so. That's why I asked you if you had ever thought about why one person might so fervently desire another."

Kim was now thoroughly disturbed. It occurred to her she might be in physical danger, possibly become a victim of sexual assault. Hamlet increased her feeling of alarm to near panic when he suddenly threw his arms around her and kissed her impetuously on the lips. She resorted to a tactic she had used on rare occasions with especially aggressive men.

"Professor Hamlet," she said, as if regretful at having to tell him bad news, "I'm having my period. Any intimacy at this time would be impractical. In fact, I must go to the bathroom right now and change my pad. I will rethink our relationship, and perhaps, in the future, I might change my mind."

Suddenly, Hamlet moved toward her. "Let me go," she cried, as he embraced her again and pressed his lips to hers.

"All right," he said. "Go."

She opened and closed the bathroom door, praying Hamlet would think her inside and accept a longer than usual stay without becoming suspicious.

She turned her attention to the cabinet. As Davis had instructed her, she inserted the screwdriver blade between the doors and pried with a twisting motion. A gap of about a quarter inch opened between the doors. She put her eye to this opening, and with her left hand, she directed the beam of the flashlight into the interior. At first she could not comprehend what she was seeing, it was so unexpected, so startlingly impossible.

Then, as her shock subsided, she was able to accept the astounding reality. Inside a glass case, behind the wooden doors, she could see the figure of a woman, lying as a corpse does, head resting on a satin pillow, body reclined upon a satin bed, arms folded across her waist.

She almost cried out at the gruesome sight but contained herself as the realization struck her. The woman in the glass case was the mirror image of herself. It was as if she, Kim Kendall, lay there in that coffin, hidden behind a padlocked cupboard, held there for reasons she could not imagine by a demented professor.

She struggled to the bathroom door, opened and closed it, and emerged in the studio to confront Hamlet.

He looked at her distraught face, her pale skin, her quivering chin, and said, "What's the matter with you? You act as if you've seen a ghost."

Struggling to keep herself from breaking down, Kim bit her lip and replied, "I'm having terrible menstrual cramps. I'm really quite ill, Professor Hamlet. Do you mind if I leave?"

She did not wait for him to answer but bolted out the door and ran through the dark street toward home.

Chapter Thirteen

It was six o'clock in the morning. They roused Hamlet from sleep and handed him the warrant.

"I have an order here entitling us to search your premises," Davis said. "This is Detective Fulford, and these are Officers Baker and Fields, who will be helping us. We will begin our search in your glass studio. If you give us the key, we won't have to force the door."

Hamlet, dressed in a bathrobe, said nothing. He appeared surprised and disoriented. Instead of showing alarm, guilt, or indignation, all the things the officers had expected, he seemed overcome by a great sadness.

Finally, pulling himself together, he said, "Can you wait until I put on some clothes? I'd like to accompany you." His voice broke, almost as if he were about to cry.

Without knowing why, Fulford felt sorry for him. Only the recollection of what Kim Kendall had found in his subterranean workshop kept her from speaking words of consolation.

Dressed, Hamlet joined them. Taking a key from a desk drawer, he said, "Shall we get this over with?"

As he unlocked the door to the old bomb shelter, he spoke again, "I know what you're after, and I will take you directly there. You are mistaken, however, in thinking I have committed a crime. If I am guilty of anything, it can only be a minor infraction."

He opened the door and ushered the officers into the studio.

"I'm afraid the court will have to be the judge of that," Davis said. "If, as you say, you know what we are after, please lead us to the body."

Hamlet said no more.

He led them through the kitchenette to the cabinet in the rear wall of the room. Taking a key from his pocket, he opened the padlock, let the lower door fall, and lifted the upper one, which he secured with a hook.

The officers stared wordlessly at what now lay exposed—the body of a beautiful young woman dressed in silk and reposing upon a bed of satin. She seemed, in Fulford's imagination, like the sleeping princess of fairy tale lore, pale and ethereal, awaiting an act of resurrection.

Davis, who, like the others, stared hypnotically at the image before him, finally roused himself and said, "I must tell you, Professor Hamlet, that stealing another person's body and hiding it away for your own purposes is indeed a crime, for which you will be held accountable."

"And I must tell you, Detective Davis, that I did not steal this body. It belongs to me. It is the body of Geraldine Hamlet, my wife."

They allowed Ralph Hamlet to eat breakfast in the police commissary, then, at nine, they brought him into an interrogation room. He had been read his rights and had been told he could have an attorney present if he wished. He waived his rights, declaring he would at all times be telling the truth and required no lawyer to coach him in doing so.

Davis began by asking, "Would you like a cup of coffee?"

Hamlet declined.

"Let's get to the heart of this matter," Davis said. "You have kept the body of your wife, Geraldine, secreted in your studio since her death?"

"Yes. Just a little over a year now."

"When did you decide you were going to keep her in your possession?"

"I made the decision immediately after her death. I loved her with a love that went beyond reason. At first, I thought I would have her preserved by freezing. I found a cryonics company that will freeze a body and store it in a mausoleum to be viewed at the family's pleasure. I thought I might use their services, but the process was terribly expensive, and their mausoleum was in California, so I decided to take care of her myself. The cabinet in which you found her is really a modified freezer. I could never bring myself to actually freeze her. It just seemed too extreme. I then discovered it was really unnecessary as long as I kept the temperature between thirty-five and forty degrees Fahrenheit."

"Did it ever occur to you that your wife might not have liked the way you were using her?" Fulford asked.

"She loved me as much as I loved her," Hamlet said. "I think, had she been aware, she would have approved."

"You couldn't have carried out your scheme alone," Davis said. "Someone must have helped you. Your wife's body had to be embalmed, very meticulously, I would think, for it to last indefinitely. And then some kind of burial ceremony had to take place to deceive family and friends about what was really happening."

"Yes," Hamlet nodded in agreement. "I was able to convince Garner Jakes, Geraldine's undertaker, to do what was a virtual mummification of the body. I paid him a handsome sum to prepare her and to certify she had been cremated. After the alleged cremation, he helped me move her to the cabinet where you found her."

Fulford found the man's ability to talk so matter-of-factly about what should have been, in her opinion, an emotion-laden narrative, disturbing. She thought he might be a victim of depression, a melancholy so deep, he was virtually numb.

She suggested to Davis they take a short break and give Hamlet a chance to drink the coffee he had finally requested. Her real purpose, however, was to confer with him about the implications of Hamlet's testimony.

They stood apart in the hallway, ignoring the passage of officers escorting miscreants in cuffs and leg irons to their dismal accounting with the law. They paid no attention to the background of discordant noise. Ralph Hamlet's narrative had driven all else from their minds.

"I think," Davis said, "we have found the murderer of Garner Jakes. When he read about the discovery of a young woman's body near Proctor Creek, Jakes, who had helped Hamlet hide the body of his wife, assumed he had begun collecting other bodies for his private enjoyment. That's a belief, incidentally, I share.

"Jakes called us thinking he could identify the body after he had met with Hamlet and forced him to reveal who the woman was. Hamlet, to avoid exposure, met Jakes at his place and murdered him. Having been in Jakes's home before, he knew Jakes owned a Japanese sword. To use it, all he had to do was drug his victim."

Fulford, who had been listening attentively to Davis's theory, but with growing skepticism, raised objections.

"Hamlet is not a true necrophiliac, Wade. There's absolutely no evidence he had intercourse with his wife's body. She was sealed in a glass case that held some kind of inert gas which, according to forensics, prevents decomposition. She and Lenin, whom millions have seen in Red Square, are kept whole in much the same way. Any rough handling, such as would occur during intercourse, would have led to rapid deterioration."

"Leda, you're no expert on sexual deviance. And forensics, to my knowledge, hasn't yet made a report on Geraldine Hamlet's remains."

"That's true, but Chris was sweet enough to give me a call just before we started questioning Hamlet."

"I forgot the two of you were such close friends," Davis said spitefully. "A quid pro quo, I suppose."

"I'll ignore that remark, Wade," Fulford said. "As for my being an expert on necrophilia, I told you I read the stuff Albert dug up on the internet. It's an impressive article. The authors cite a study in which one hundred and twenty-two cases of alleged necrophilia were examined. They concluded that only fifty of those people could be classified as true necrophiliacs. The pseudo-necrophiliacs included people who had an attraction for corpses that was not erotic, and those who, although they were attracted sexually, engaged in no actual contact with a corpse."

"I'm impressed, Leda," Davis said sarcastically. "You're quite a scholar. A real nose for the books."

She had not seen him so mean-spirited before and wondered about the cause. Jealousy seemed likely, but was it jealousy of her friendship with Chris McCalmon, or was it because she had often disagreed with him about the case? As for the latter eventuality, she had no intention of arguing any view except one she truly believed.

"I don't think you're impressed, Wade. I think you're pissed because you'd like to hang a murder rap on Hamlet regardless. Well, I'm sure Hamlet didn't kill Jakes. It would take a hell of a lot of twisted logic to make me think he did. Do you think he killed Donnie Grey, too? Grey was killed by the person who dumped Mrs. Wills's body at Proctor Creek. If Hamlet had her body in his possession, where did he keep her? There was room for only one body in his bomb shelter.

"And Julia Wills's body had been raped. Hamlet, not being a true necrophiliac, would never have done that. If he were going to rape anyone, it would have been Kim Kendall. You know why he came on to her so strong? She's almost a clone of his wife, and she's alive. Being alive, she was sexually available. His wife, poor dead thing, was not."

She looked at Davis in a challenging manner. He stared back defiantly but spoke less assertively.

"Well, you've got your theory and I've got mine. I think Hamlet's a true necrophiliac who used his wife's body as a visual stimulus to get himself sexually excited. Then he satisfied his lust with Julia Wills's corpse, which he had hidden away elsewhere."

"Okay," said Fulford. "You find where he kept Julia Wills's body hidden, and I'll go along with you."

Davis made no attempt to conceal his impatience with her. "Let's get back to Hamlet," he said shortly.

When they returned to the interrogation room, Hamlet was pacing the floor nervously. Davis went after him vigorously. "Sit down, Professor Hamlet. Isn't it true that Garner Jakes threatened to tell the police you had your wife's body secreted in your house, and, in order to silence him, you killed him?"

Hamlet shook his head in denial. "What an absurd idea. While I would have been most unhappy to have my secret revealed, exposure would not have injured me enough to warrant my killing Jakes."

"Perhaps so," Davis continued, "but if Jakes knew, or suspected, you had stolen and violated the body of Julia Wills and threatened to tell the police, that would have given you enough reason for murder."

For the first time, Hamlet looked genuinely alarmed. Wiping his brow with a tissue and drumming his fingers anxiously on the chair arm, he denied the accusation vigorously.

"I had nothing to do with the abduction of Julia Wills's body. How could I have managed to break into a mortuary, remove a body, and substitute bags of fertilizer for it? The person who could have done that most easily, Detective Davis, would be an undertaker. Have you ever thought that Mr. Jakes himself could have stolen her body?"

"It has occurred to us. Our position, however, is that Jakes was murdered by the person who abducted Mrs. Wills's body. We think you're that person. You went to Jakes's house after he told you he was going to the police, put a sedative in his coffee, and murdered him with a sword you had previously seen hanging on his living room wall."

Hamlet made a despondent gesture. When he spoke, however, his voice was still defiant. "I have never been in Jakes's home. I never had any reason to go there. All of our meetings took place in my studio. He came there first to help me manage the placement of my wife's body. After that, I never saw him again until he came to one of my leaded glass exhibits and was so impressed, he asked if I would give him instruction in the art. I agreed. He had been to my studio for lessons perhaps five or six times before he was murdered. Never, in any of those visits, did he bring up his having helped me with the disposition of my wife's body. Nor did he make any reference to Julia Wills or suggest, even in the most roundabout way, I had anything to do with her abduction. I swear, sir, that is the God's truth."

Fulford was impressed. She thought he sounded sincere, but Davis was unmoved.

"The truth is often abused in God's name," he said somewhat sententiously. "You had the motive and opportunity to kill Jakes. That makes you our prime suspect. Where were you the night before last, Professor Hamlet, between the hours of eight and midnight?"

Hamlet shook his head ruefully. "I was working in my studio. Unfortunately, there is no one who can back me up on that. I was alone. I'm sure you won't believe me."

Davis smiled grimly. "You're right, Professor Hamlet, I don't believe you. I'm obliged to tell you, you will be charged with Garner Jakes's murder."

Chapter Fourteen

Though she admitted that Ralph Hamlet could possibly be Jakes's murderer, Leda Fulford was convinced he was not. She resolved to uncover the real killer. Earlier she was convinced that Jakes himself had stolen Julia Wills's body and killed Grey when Grey found him out. But when Jakes was killed, she had been obliged to rethink everything. Now the only person who made sense as a possible suspect was the unknown man Jakes had told his father about, the man who, as Jakes put it, was engaged in unethical, possibly criminal behavior. Could he not have been referring to the necrophiliac who stole and violated Julia Wills's body?

If that were the case, the culprit had to be one of Jakes's friends and acquaintances. Baxter Cawthon had given her the names of two people Jakes knew well: Gwendolyn Smith, a female student in the Burial Science School, and Richard Cheatham, his assistant. He had also told her of Hercules Brown, with whom Jakes had a minor altercation. Brown was no longer available, having gone back to Alabama, but she could locate and question the other two.

She chose to interview Smith first, a decision that required her to drive to Marietta. In the forty minutes it took to get to her destination, her thoughts strayed to Wade Davis. She felt hurt when he had spoken so spitefully about her knowledge of necrophilia, a knowledge she had gained by several hours of laborious study. But in spite of the hurt, she found her affection for him increasing. His actions, she felt, were motivated by his jealousy of Chris McCalmon. How could she let him know that Chris was no threat to him? Chris was a sweet and lovable guy, but he stirred no spark of passion in her. She would have to let the Davis connection, as she thought of it momentarily, develop as fate would steer it and hope for the best.

Gwendolyn Smith received her graciously. A tall, slender woman with gray eyes, a dimpled smile, ruddy cheeks, and straight black hair, she reminded Fulford of a grade school teacher she once had. But there was nothing of the classroom disciplinarian about her. Tentative, unassuming, and hesitant, she lacked assurance.

"I have never talked to the police before," she said with a shy smile. "You can imagine my concern when you called. Then, when you told me you preferred not to discuss the nature of your visit over the phone, my heartbeat went wild. I imagined all sorts of things."

Fulford hastened to reassure her. "You know about Garner Jakes's murder," she began, intending to add that she was making a routine investigation of that event. But before she could finish the sentence, Smith's hands flew upward and clutched her throat, her face flushed with fright, and she appeared so agitated, Fulford thought she was about to faint.

"Oh! My God!" she said. "You think I had something to do with that?"

Fulford, astonished by the woman's reaction, took her by the hand and repeated, "No, no, no! I don't think you had anything to do with the murder. But you were at one time acquainted with Jakes, and I thought you might have some information about him that could help us."

"Then you don't know about our meeting last Sunday?" Jones said, still agitated.

It was Fulford's turn to be surprised. Baxter Cawthon had led her to believe that Jakes and Smith had known one another only briefly, and never intimately.

"I thought you and Jakes only saw each other while you were students at Cawthon's school."

"That's true. We had three or four dates at that time and then drifted apart. I hadn't seen him since graduation, until last Sunday when, quite by accident, I ran across him in the food court of the Lennox Mall. He seemed glad to see me and suggested we have a cup of coffee together. We talked for perhaps forty-five minutes, that's all. I don't think anything we said could be relevant to his murder."

Fulford nodded. "I'm sure you're right, but I would appreciate your telling me, as fully as you can remember, what you talked about."

"Well, each of us wanted to know how the other was doing in business. I think Garner was especially anxious to know if my being a woman was a handicap. I told him I thought at first it put off some clients, but that prejudice toward me seemed to be tapering off. He said he was glad because he always felt I had a great talent for the profession. Those were welcome words to me, and I was pleased to hear him say them.

"We talked about our school days and some of the other students who studied with us—"

"I'm sorry to interrupt," Fulford said, "but did you know anything about a run-in he had with a student named Hercules Brown?"

"No, ma'am. I don't think we ever had a student with that name. If we had, I'm sure I'd remember him."

"Okay. Why don't you go on."

"We both fondly remembered a fellow student named Randall Strickland because he spoke so honestly and humorously about his motives for becoming a mortician. 'Why not?' he'd say. 'It's the world's securest job. You can't lose. The demand is constant. Everybody dies. And whenever there's a natural disaster, like a hurricane or an earthquake, business really booms.' "

"I suspect," Fulford said, "not everyone was enchanted by that kind of talk."

"You'd be surprised. Being reminded daily of your own mortality isn't easy. Some people avoid being depressed by resorting to sick humor. Strickland used to come up with ridiculous stuff like his 'Sensitive Morticians Scale of Desirable Stiffs.' I won't offend you with the content of his list," she said, smiling in recollection, "but it was clever in a ghoulish way."

"I'm sure it was," Fulford said. She turned the conversation in a direction she hoped might offer some support for an explanation of Jakes's murder that was growing in her mind.

"Did Garner by any chance talk about Baxter Cawthon during your conversation?"

"We both spoke of him. I think all of his students admired Mr. Cawthon. He was very supportive of me. I think I may have been one of the first women to graduate from his school. He often expressed the hope that more women would be attracted to the profession. He liked Garner very much. He kept in touch with him after graduation, helped him get started, and according to Garner, visited his establishment often to see if he could be of help."

"I suppose Garner had nothing but praise for him."

"It's curious you should say that. I thought I detected a hint or two of reservation in his remarks about Baxter. Nothing I could put my finger on, but there was an attitude of reservation, as if something were troubling him. He reminded me of a son who had discovered something shameful about a father he admired very much."

"He didn't give you any idea what that something was?"

"No. I'm not sure if the impression I had was real, or if I just imagined it."

It occurred to Fulford that, had Jakes and Cawthon been as close as Gwendolyn Smith said they were, Cawthon could have told her much more about Jakes's affairs than he did when she interviewed him. And she was bothered by the story of Hercules Brown. Surely Gwendolyn would have remembered him if he had been a fellow student. Brown, she thought, could have been an invention of Cawthon's, told for some devious purpose she did not understand. But then, perhaps not. Cawthon said Brown had left the school after only a few days in residence. Smith might never have had a chance to see him.

"Can you think of anything at all," Fulford asked, "that Jakes said or did that might suggest he was in trouble?"

"He made one remark," she replied. "I thought nothing of it at the time, but now, given what has happened to him, it seems strange. When we were leaving, he said, 'I hope we see one another again soon. In a few days, I'll have an interesting story to tell you. Perhaps you'll even read about me in the papers.' I thought he was joking and didn't press him for an explanation. Afterward, I assumed he meant he was going to conduct the funeral of some prominent person."

She told Davis of her interview with Gwendolyn Smith. He listened to her account without enthusiasm and was openly derogatory when she sketched her new resolution of the case.

"Why complicate things by imagining additional suspects? Ralph Hamlet is our man. In spite of your reservations about his sexuality, I think he's a true necrophiliac and quite capable, with Jakes's help, of stealing and holding Julia Wills's body. I think if we lean on him hard enough, he'll break down and confess."

"You'd better be right," Fulford said, "because if he doesn't, you'll have a hell of a time convicting him. All you've got against him is the possession of his wife's body. You have no evidence he abused it and nothing at all to connect him to Julia Wills."

He gave her a superior smile. "Not true. While you were out talking with Gwendolyn Smith and drumming up false leads, we true believers discovered Hamlet had a summer cottage on Richard B.

Russell Lake. We ran out there immediately, and guess what we found?"

Fulford, anticipating a devastating revelation, refused to be drawn out. She stared stolidly at Davis and waited for his disclosure.

"We found four fifty-pound bags of fertilizer, the same brand as the two that were in Julia Wills's coffin. They appear to have been lying around in his shed for a long time. Manufacturers put code numbers on fertilizer bags to indicate the batch they were filled with. Those bags were filled a year ago and are marked with the same numbers as the bags taken from Julia Wills's coffin. Neat, huh?"

Fulford was quick to object. "Wade, have you stopped to consider that probably hundreds of bags of fertilizer are filled from the same batch? Given that fact, it would be hard to tie Hamlet to the two bags found in Wills's coffin."

"Maybe. But when you ask what Hamlet was doing with two hundred pounds of fertilizer at a summer place that has maybe four thousand square feet of lawn, you grow suspicious."

"Did you ask him why he had it?"

"He's got a lawyer now who told him not to talk or answer questions. But that's not all we found, Leda. In a file cabinet we found a folder filled with newspaper clippings. One batch consisted of articles, collected from several papers, about the wrangling over the demand of Julia Wills's parents to have their daughter's body exhumed on the assumption her husband had poisoned her. Then there was another batch relating to our discovery of a dismembered arm, the tying of the arm to the body found at Proctor Creek, and the murder of Donovan Grey.

"It appears Professor Hamlet was vitally interested in the possibility of a judge granting an exhumation order in the Wills case. Is it stretching reason too far to suppose that, being aware of the likelihood of an exhumation order, he decided to get rid of Julia's body before the authorities discovered it was missing and mounted a determined search for it? Is it too unreasonable to suppose he disposed of the body at Proctor Creek? That he knew Donovan Grey had seen him and murdered him to keep him quiet?"

"I still think you're wrong, Wade. There's no physical evidence linking Hamlet with Julia Wills's body. Without it, everything's conjecture. I don't think a jury would buy the story."

She was beginning to feel less confident, however, in her own theory. The connection between the man she suspected and the abduction of Wills's body was tenuous at best. And solid proof was lacking to connect him with the murders of Donovan Grey and Garner Jakes. She hoped, in the next day or so, to establish those connections, to demonstrate motivation and opportunity beyond a reasonable doubt. But for the moment, she felt the need to mend fences between herself and Davis.

"I don't mean to be obstinate about this, Wade. You build a plausible case against Hamlet. If I can't make a better case against my man, I'll shut up and support you."

Davis grinned and nodded approvingly. "Okay. We'll call a truce. We're each committed to a theory. Let's see how each one proves out. In the meantime," he put a hand on her arm, "how about another date? Friday night the 'Wheel of Fortune' is going to originate from the Fox Theater. Wouldn't you love to see Vanna White turn a few letters?"

The proposal put her in an embarrassing situation. She tried to think of a graceful way to tell him what she must. She failed.

"I'm sorry, Wade, I've promised to go out with Chris McCalmon."

Davis was hurt and responded rudely, "What is it with you two? You going steady? I should warn you, Leda, Chris is not a one-woman man. You'll end up just another one of his conquests."

"Damn it, Wade, you're being vicious. I thought Chris was a friend of yours. Is that the way you talk about all your friends?"

"I'm thinking of your welfare, that's all."

"I doubt that. You're thinking of yourself. I don't understand why you are trying to drive me into a commitment I'm not ready for. God, we've only known each other a few weeks, and you want me to forsake all others for your benefit. I'm not going to do it."

"Okay," he said apologetically, "I get the message. You don't have to beat me over the head."

He looked so dejected, she felt her heart soften toward him. "I like you, Wade, I really do. You're a sweet, attractive man." She reached out and let her hand softly stroke his cheek. "But ease up a little, will you? Give it some time."

Davis, whose head had been bowed in dejection, now looked up with a smile. "I'll try. Honestly, I will."

She answered his smile with one of her own. "I assure you, I will not become just another one of Chris's conquests."

Chapter Fifteen

Had Richard Cheatham not been an undertaker, he might have been mistaken for a distinguished scientist. He had the bearing of a Nobel Prize winner, exhibiting an aura of competence in an esoteric field that allows one, with appropriate modesty, to look down upon the common herd. He greeted Fulford with easy familiarity.

"Ms. Fulford, how nice to see you." He paused, scanning her with frankly sexual interest. "I never knew police officers came in such attractive packages."

"I'm sure you mean that as a compliment," Fulford responded. "If I dealt with you as a lawbreaker, however, I suspect you'd find me considerably less attractive."

"Let us hope that never happens," Cheatham said. "Your present visit does not assume lawbreaking on my part, does it?"

"I am here to ask a few questions about your deceased boss, Garner Jakes. That's all."

"A sad business, Garner's death. He was a good man. For him to come to a violent end is almost unbelievable. As far as I know, he had no enemies."

"You describe him as a good man. Would you also say he was an easy man to get along with?"

"Very easy. He always seemed eager to please."

"Do you think that, just to be compliant, he might have been talked into something that was, well, unwise? Perhaps unethical? Something that might have led to his murder?"

"I'm not sure what you have in mind. I know Garner would never do anything unethical, nor would he let anyone talk him into doing something shady. A mortician learns from a client's remains evidence of unsavory things. Physical abuse, alcoholism, venereal diseases, and so on. An unethical person might try to exploit that knowledge.

I'm sure Garner never did. He was always sympathetic, almost to a fault, with the family of the deceased. He would bend over backward to ease their grief. He respected their wishes and their privacy tenaciously."

"That fits with what we've been told by others," Fulford said. "We're concerned, however, that he may have had a run-in with an unknown member of the undertaker's profession. Can you tell me who in this business he had a close relationship with?"

"He was not a gregarious man, but he did belong to a countywide professional organization. We both did. In that context, I've seen him lunching with several people. Most often with a man named Bruce Grimshaw, who has a mortuary in Iron Mountain. But I would hardly call their association a friendship. I never saw them together outside a convention meeting."

"What about Baxter Cawthon?"

"That's a different matter. Baxter took a liking to Garner when Garner was a student in his school. He helped him with tuition, and I've heard Garner hint that he helped him get a loan to set up his business. I know Cawthon visited here often. He would help Garner whenever he had doubts about how to deal with a client's complaint, or when Garner got sick. Garner had weak lungs and couldn't give up smoking. As a result, he suffered most of the time from a debilitating bronchitis, and once in a while he would be laid up with a mild form of pneumonia."

"That's when Cawthon would step in?"

"Yes. More than once he's helped out. He used to scold Garner about his smoking, and Garner would promise to quit. But he never did."

"I'm surprised he didn't rely more on you rather than calling on Cawthon."

"Most of the time he did. I've helped him through more than one of his mini-crises. But occasionally I'd be under the weather at the same time he was."

"Did that happen often?"

"No. I think the last time was about a year ago. The reason I remember is that Garner had been entrusted with the burial of that woman who has recently received so much publicity, Julia Wills. Garner had pneumonia, and though he was not hospitalized, he was confined to bed at home. I had a bad case of the flu and couldn't get out of bed. Cawthon stepped in and handled the whole thing for us.

I'm glad he was in charge, otherwise Garner and I might have been suspected of playing tricks with her body."

"Are you suggesting Baxter Cawthon might have substituted bags of fertilizer for Wills's body?"

"It's possible, isn't it? Though why he would do such a thing is beyond me. What would he want with a dead woman's body?"

"Did anyone else stand in for you and Garner when you were ill or on vacation?"

"Grimshaw did once. That was for the burial of some man whose name I don't remember."

"He never helped out with the burial of a woman?"

"Never."

Fulford felt her pulse increase as the import of Cheatham's testimony sank in. Was this the evidence she had hoped to find? Cawthon's presence in Jakes's mortuary at the time Julia Wills was buried could be no more than a coincidence. Something like the fact that Ralph Hamlet had two hundred pounds of fertilizer in his possession of the type found in Wills's coffin. Neither was definitive proof.

"Has anyone else talked to you about this case?"

"Herbert Wills called me just yesterday and wanted all the details concerning Julia Wills's burial. It seem his in-laws insisted on making all the funeral arrangements."

"Did you tell him Cawthon stood in for you and Jakes?"

"I did."

She could think of only one more question to ask Cheatham. "Did Julia Wills have on her wedding ring when she was buried?"

"I couldn't say for sure. But in most cases, married women wear their wedding bands. I can think of only one exception in all the time I've been in the business."

As she got up to leave, Cheatham gave her another of his explicitly erotic looks and said, "I hope I'm not being offensive, Ms. Fulford, but it would be nice if we could see each other again. Could I telephone you?"

She gave him a cold stare. "Sorry. My line is always busy, I'm afraid."

Herbert Wills was angry. He faced Davis and Fulford belligerently, a man full of righteous anger, a man wronged, a man seeking redress for heinous grievances.

"You withheld from me the truth about my wife's abduction and what happened to her," he charged. "I didn't find out the facts until your forensics people discovered no sign of poison, and Judge Tremont ordered her body released to me." He paused momentarily, almost inarticulate.

Fulford steeled herself against the censure to come. She glanced at Davis and saw regret stamped on his features. Both were resigned to Wills's condemnation.

"When your medical officer surrendered Julia to me, I was stunned," he continued. "She had been mutilated, a fact the two of you never told me." His next words were spoken with an air of incredulity. They were uttered with insistent, harsh emphasis. "Her arm had been cut off." Tears of outrage and frustration ran down his cheeks.

"Why didn't you tell me that? Did you have some idiotic notion I needed to be shielded from the truth? What else have you hidden from me?"

Davis was dismayed at the question. Chris McCalmon, it appeared, had not told him the worst. That responsibility now lay on him and his colleague. He began defensively, "It is not departmental policy to reveal details about a body's condition when, under court order, a forensic examination is being conducted." That was not the exact truth, but Davis was not above hiding a questionable decision behind alleged regulations. "We intended to inform you of her amputated arm the minute the forensic examination was complete. And we did that."

He did not mention the fact that the mutilation of Julia Wills's body could scarcely have been concealed. He saw no reason to rob a necessity of its virtue.

Wills was not placated. His face still flushed, his hands still shaking, his voice still agitated, he demanded, "I insist you tell me what else you have concealed from me."

Davis sighed and capitulated. "This will be terribly painful to you, Mr. Wills, and horrifying. I personally see no point in revealing it, but since you insist, I have no choice. Your wife's body was in the hands of a necrophiliac, who, at least on one occasion, raped her."

Herbert Wills's face contorted in pain. He bent forward, apparently seized by cramps. A drop of liquid dripped from his nose, as if he had inhaled some corrosive gas and was about to choke. He struggled to regain his composure and, at last, was able to speak.

"Who could have done that? A monster, surely. No human being would do such a thing. He deserves to die. I could kill him myself." A tic trembled in his cheek as he struggled to think of an appropriate punishment. "I could put a knife in his belly and twist it like a corkscrew."

He glared at the detectives, a man frenzied by thoughts of unspeakable offense. As he listened to Wills's threats and observed his agitated behavior, Davis believed the man would be quite capable of carrying out the violent reprisals he uttered.

"Have you caught this man, this . . . beast?"

"We've arrested a man named Ralph Hamlet," Davis said evenly, ignoring Wills's agitated manner. "The evidence linking him to your wife's abduction is circumstantial. My colleague, Ms. Fulford, believes he is not guilty and is investigating other leads. We assure you we are working on the case diligently, and the man who violated your wife's body will be caught and punished."

"Punished?" Wills said bitterly. "A good lawyer, a plea of insanity, a few months in a psychiatric hospital, then freedom. Is that a punishment fit for his crime?"

"You must trust the court to dispense justice, Mr. Wills. Don't forget, the man will face murder charges in addition to the offense against your wife. I am confident he will get a long prison term, perhaps even a death sentence."

"I wish I shared your belief," Wills said. "Unfortunately, I do not." He rose abruptly and left the room.

"He's boiling with hate," Fulford observed. "And I don't blame him. He's had a lot on his plate these last few days."

"Yeah," Davis said. "He's in a state. I hope he doesn't do something foolish."

Chapter Sixteen

"I've been expecting you, Ms. Fulford," Cawthon said, as he ushered her into his fancy office, which was situated in one corner of his laboratory. The lab, although it was early morning, was now empty of students and specimens.

"Is today a holiday?" Fulford asked.

"I'm tempted to reply, 'Death never takes a holiday,' but I'll refrain from such banalities out of deference to your mission."

"Very thoughtful of you," Fulford said sarcastically.

He sat down opposite her and looked at her with an approving glance. "No, it is not a holiday. I simply wished to keep my time open for your convenience. You're a smart woman. I felt sure you would eventually become aware of the role Garner Jakes played in the stealing of Julia Wills's body and come to me about it. Until just recently, because I liked Garner so much, I couldn't face the unpleasant fact that he had manipulated me into being an unwitting accomplice in his scheme."

Fulford, who had one objective—to lure Cawthon into making admissions of fact that she could use against him—was dismayed that he had taken the initiative away by reciting his own version of events. There was little she could do, for the moment, but listen to his story.

"Are you contending Garner Jakes stole Julia Wills's body?"

"To me, it's quite obvious. I can't see any other explanation. I must say, I thought you would have tumbled to it almost at once. In addition, I say he must have murdered Donovan Grey."

He paused, nodding sagely, as if offering her a lesson in elementary logic. "It stands to reason. From what I read in the papers, the person who killed Grey did so because Grey saw him with Julia Wills's body at Proctor Creek. The person Grey saw was Jakes. Garner had to get rid of the body because of the approaching exhumation. He was in the process of dismembering her when Grey saw him. He had no alternative but to kill Grey for fear he would expose him."

"An interesting theory, Mr. Cawthon," Fulford said. "However, may I ask the name of the unknown person who killed Jakes and why that person resorted to murder?"

"Again, it's as plain as the nose on your face," Cawthon replied. "I'm surprised the identity of the murderer didn't occur to you at once. Who else would have the motive, the hatred equal to the task, except Herbert Wills, Julia's husband. He would understandably be filled with rage at the man who stole his wife's body and raped her. Revenge is one of the most common motives for murder. As a detective, you know that better than anyone."

"Revenge is not the only motive for murder, Mr. Cawthon. Moreover, I remind you that, in my opinion, the facts of the case may be explained quite well by another, more convincing theory. Listen to my version of events, if you will."

"By all means," Cawthon said. "Fire away." He appeared to be enjoying the clash of opinion. His smug expression suggested he had no fear of being held to account for the murders of Grey and Jakes.

"Let's assume a hypothetical Mr. X," Fulford said. "A person involved in the undertaking business who, as a result of constant exposure from his work, or from an innate disposition, develops an unnatural sexual attraction to dead bodies. To feed his appetite, he removes the bodies of young women who are consigned to his care and hides them in his establishment. When he has lost interest in a body, he disposes of it by burial in some remote place, or by dismemberment."

"May I interrupt?" Cawthon asked. "Why in the world wouldn't he just cremate the bodies?"

"Because he doesn't have a crematorium. Mr. X is not a bona fide undertaker, though you might have assumed that from what I said. He is the master of a school that teaches embalming, not cremation."

"Someone like Baxter Cawthon, I presume?" His voice was heavy with sarcasm.

"If the shoe fits," Fulford replied, angry at Cawthon's arrogance. "Let me continue. About a year ago, Mr. X gets a call from Garner Jakes, who is charged with the burial of Julia Wills. Jakes is ill, too ill to take care of the Wills burial. He asks his old mentor for help. Mr. X agrees to do the job, not realizing Wills is an incredibly beautiful young woman. When he sees her, he is captivated. He must have her for his depraved appetite. He steals her from her coffin and keeps her hidden in his laboratory until, discovering her grave is about to be opened, he acts hastily to dispose of her. He carries her to Proctor Creek, and after violating her one last time, starts to dismember her.

"While engaged in this gruesome task, he discovers he is being watched by a naive youth. He frightens the boy off but fears the boy will expose him. He lures him back to Proctor Creek and murders him. The boy's feminine features and graceful body excite him sexually, and he commits an act of sodomy."

"An unwholesome character by your account," Cawthon said. "I'm beginning to feel some resentment toward you, Detective Fulford, for your insinuations."

"Mr. X is indeed unwholesome," Fulford continued, "and becomes more so because he now resorts to a second murder. This time his brutality is visited upon a friend, Garner Jakes, who, suspecting his involvement in the abduction of Julia Wills and the subsequent murder of Donovan Grey, challenges him. Mr. X, denying any involvement in the crimes, urges Jakes to meet him, promising to reveal the real culprit. Instead, he drugs his friend's coffee and savagely kills him with a sword."

She paused, her eyes resting on Cawthon's face in unconcealed loathing.

He returned her stare brazenly. "What am I to say to this fanciful tale, Ms. Fulford? Surely you don't expect me to credit as truth a tissue of suppositions, guesswork, and malicious inferences. I remind you that, in a court of law, evidence is required to sustain criminal charges. I have not heard one iota of evidence in anything you have said."

A moment of concern dampened Fulford's satisfaction at having outlined her hypothesis so clearly and forcefully. Cawthon had spotted the weakness in it and had shown his disdain. Her case, she was painfully aware, was almost entirely circumstantial. She hoped forensics would be able to bolster some of her allegations.

But would a grand jury return an indictment with no other evidence but bits of fiber, flecks of paint, and DNA analyses? In the midst of doubt, she rejoiced in one fact. Cawthon had impeached his own theory by unwittingly mixing up the chronology of events.

"Sorry to disturb your complacency, Mr. Cawthon, but I have not revealed all the evidence our forensics people have accumulated linking Mr. X to the murders of Grey and Jakes. Those linkages will come out in court. It will also come out in court that Mr. X's version of the case, in which Mr. Wills is cast as the murderer, is negated by the fact that Wills was not aware of the way his wife's body had been violated until after the death of Garner Jakes. Hence, he would have had no motive for killing Jakes."

Cawthon seemed undisturbed by Fulford's remarks. His chubby, benign face remained calm. If he felt any anxiety, he did not show it.

"I assume," he said, acting like a man whose patience has been sorely tried, "nothing more is to be gained by prolonging this interview. Shall we bring this charade to an end?"

He stood up and signaled Fulford to do the same. "I'm sure it has not escaped your notice that you have accomplished absolutely nothing by this attack upon my character. If you had any sense of shame, you would apologize to me."

Fulford's laugh was incredulous. "Your gall is unbelievable. You'll be hearing from me again."

Cawthon sighed, as if he had been disappointed in a cruel way. "I suppose one cannot expect civility from a policewoman. I'll not let your behavior keep me from being a gentleman, however. Come, I'll walk you to your car. I trust your next visit will be more courteous. I despise these accusational meetings. They generate bad feelings."

Although Fulford intended to make a scathing rejoinder to Cawthon's insolence and remove herself from his odious presence as quickly as possible, a totally unexpected event intervened.

Out of a car parked near her own, a man emerged, a man fierce of eye and maniacal of manner, who advanced upon them like a wild beast. In his right hand he held a semiautomatic pistol, which he leveled menacingly at Cawthon and Fulford.

"Ms. Fulford," he commanded, "unholster your weapon and let it drop to the ground. If you don't, I will be forced to shoot you."

Fulford recognized Herbert Wills and suspected, with foreboding, what he was up to. She recalled his frenzied emotion when she and Davis had told him about the abuse of his wife's body. Having learned from Cheatham that Cawthon, rather than Jakes, had conducted his wife's funeral, he put two and two together. He intended now to have his revenge.

"Herbert," she said in a pleading voice, "don't do this. It's wrong. You know how wrong it is." But, intimidated by Wills's emotional state and wary of his flourished weapon, she reluctantly fumbled her gun from its holster and let it drop.

Cawthon, terrified and trembling, tried to slip behind Fulford's car. He had moved no more than a few inches when Wills fired a shot that struck the pavement near his feet and ricocheted into the air with a sickening whine. Cawthon froze.

"Watch yourself, you bastard. Play your cards right and you may survive this encounter. Another misstep, however, and you're dead." He turned to Fulford. "Ms. Fulford, I have no wish to harm you, but if you interfere with me, I'll have no choice. I'll not debate with you the rightness or wrongness of my action. I think beyond such simple labels. All I want is justice."

He advanced a few steps toward them, holding the gun steadily pointed at Cawthon's chest. If he fired now, Fulford knew he could not possibly miss killing the man. A tragedy seemed about to happen, but she could think of no way to stop it. She voiced one more appeal.

"Herbert, if you shoot this man, you will go to jail for a long time. Don't do it. He's not worth it."

"I won't shoot him," Wills replied, "if he complies with one simple condition—that he get down on his knees, confess what he has done, and beg my forgiveness."

He advanced toward Cawthon, staring hatefully into his face. "Last year, when you stood in for Garner Jakes at my wife's funeral, you removed her body and hid her away to satisfy your loathsome perversion. The thought of what you did to her drives me crazy. I can barely restrain myself from smashing your face with this pistol."

He raised his arm as if to carry out his threat. Cawthon, who had begun to sweat profusely, wiped his face with his sleeve, but he had courage enough to be defiant.

"I deny your assertion," he said. "I deny, before you make them, any other slanderous charges. Why don't you put that gun away and get out of here before you do something stupid?"

Wills's face contorted. He raised his weapon again in a menacing way and advanced a step toward Cawthon. Cawthon, in fright and desperation, leaped upon him. He seized Wills by the arm, and the two men struggled for possession of the gun. Writhing and twisting, they fell to the ground.

Fulford seized Wills by the collar and tried to pull him away. He kicked her in the stomach. She fell backward, hitting her head on the pavement. Momentarily stunned, she struggled to her knees, but before she could regain her feet, she heard a shot. The two men stopped struggling. Both Wills and Cawthon lay motionless. Presently, like a man crippled by arthritis, Herbert Wills stood up, the pistol still in his hand. He looked at the gun as if it were a strange, unrecognizable thing, then handed it to Fulford.

In a voice strained with misery and remorse, he said, "I'm afraid I've killed him."

Fulford, looking at the red stain seeping through Cawthon's shirt, replied, "Yes, Herbert, I'm afraid you have."

Chapter Seventeen

At one o'clock, having finished lunch, Davis and Fulford returned to division headquarters and divided the labor of report writing, assigning the Hamlet episode to Davis, the Cawthon-Wills affair to Fulford. They set to work.

"I hope we can be done by six," Davis said. "I'd like to see how Channel Twelve handles the story."

"Me, too. Eye Witness news reports are models of objectivity."

They worked without interruption for an hour and a half, then Davis's phone rang. When he responded, he heard the voice of Hal, the switchboard operator, who bore the title of communications specialist. Hal, a lighthearted fellow who believed no routine message should be delivered routinely, always managed to transmit a communication loaded with inconsequential baggage.

"Your lady friend is on the line," he told Davis. "You want to talk to her, or are you out?"

"Which one of my many lady friends are we talking about?"

"The fish lady. Or should I say the fish person. Whatever. The one who snags cut-off arms."

"Ah! McAllister. Put her on." He signaled for Fulford to listen in.

McAllister's first words were a reproach. "I love the way you left me out of the loop," she said. "You promised to keep me informed. So why do I have to read about Hamlet and Cawthon in the papers?"

Davis wanted to tell her he had enough work to keep himself busy without wasting time bringing her up to date on the case, but he refrained out of respect for her good intentions and for the help she had given in the past.

"You probably got from the papers a fuller account of events than I could have given you by phone," he said. "The relationships among the people involved were pretty complex. The reporters did a good job of tracing them."

"Well, I forgive you. I suppose you've been too busy to humor a civic-minded lady. Just don't forget, you wouldn't have had this remarkable case if I hadn't brought you that girl's arm. Look at all the publicity you're getting."

"I assure you, I'll never forget your contribution, Ms. McAllister, though I'm not sure I'm grateful."

"You should be. Crime's your profession. Like any other professional, you should be thankful when you get new business."

Davis gave a short laugh and winked at Fulford. "I could point out some flaws in that analogy if I chose."

"Please don't. I didn't call to argue any fine points of meaning. I called to offer some information I think you would like to have."

She paused, expecting a response from Davis. He said nothing, and she went on.

"I'm sure you've asked yourself this question: If Baxter Cawthon cut off Julia Wills's arm, wrapped it in came, and threw it into the Chattahoochee, where did he get the came? You never found any at his home or at his school, did you?"

"No, we didn't. As a matter of fact, the question has been bugging me, but I've shelved it. In any investigation, odd, unexplainable facts crop up. Things that never get resolved. In this instance, it makes no difference. Cawthon's still guilty as hell."

"Granted. Wouldn't it be satisfying, though, if you knew where he got it?"

"It would be, and I assume you know or you wouldn't have called."

"Remember way back when I gave you the names of a couple of crafts shops that handled came?"

"I do. Art's Crafts and Bernhardt's Glass."

"They were just to help you get started. I assumed you would contact other glass shops in the city."

"We did."

"But not Atlanta Stained Glass?"

"It was run by three women who didn't sell came retail. We saw no point in questioning them."

"You should have. Some time ago, Cawthon commissioned them to do a couple of windows for his school. Insisted the work be done on site and was willing to pay the extra cost. While the women from Atlanta Stained Glass were on the premises, a bundle of came strips disappeared. Twenty strips. Cawthon blamed students or employ ees for the theft. He refused to make an issue of it and paid Atlanta Glass for the loss."

"So," Davis said, "if he planned to dismember Julia Wills's body and weigh the pieces down with came, he had enough to do the job."

"Exactly. He could even have sunk her torso in one piece if he wrapped it in enough came. I suspect he ditched the unused strips somewhere near Proctor Creek. You ought to go and have a look sometime."

"I'll do that," Davis said. "First chance I get."

They sat in Fillmore's office watching the six o'clock news on TV. The anchor, a good-looking blonde woman with an assured manner, promised her listeners that the report on the Cawthon killing, a carefully researched "in depth" effort, would be one of the most bizarre stories ever uncovered by the station's investigative reporters. She added a warning that much of the material was of a nature so explicit that parents might not wish their children to view it.

Davis nibbled on a ragged fingernail and looked sourly at his companions.

"Get ready, folks," he said. "Our friend is about to give the police a hard time. She'll really lay it on you, Leda."

"Early this morning," the anchor said, "the director of the Atlanta School of Burial Science, Baxter Cawthon, was gunned down in the school's parking lot. Cawthon had just been questioned by Detective Leda Fulford of Homicide Division on suspicion of having engaged in alleged acts of necrophilia and murder. He was accompanying the detective to her car when a man, later identified as Herbert Wills, leapt from a nearby vehicle and threatened the pair with an automatic pistol. In an emotional tirade, he accused Cawthon of having stolen his wife's body some fourteen months earlier as she lay in her coffin awaiting burial. He further charged that Cawthon then concealed her preserved body in his laboratory, where he periodically fondled and sexually violated it. Wills told Cawthon he sought revenge for this abominable behavior.

"Fulford, a newly appointed homicide detective, was disarmed by Wills and forced to look on helplessly as he and Cawthon argued and Cawthon, in desperation, tried to seize Wills's gun. As the two men struggled, Fulford tried but was unable to separate them. Her clumsy effort resulted in her being knocked to the pavement. Before she could recover her senses, Wills fired his gun, hitting Cawthon in the chest. Cawthon died instantly.

"After the killing, Fulford was able to take Wills into custody. He was later charged with second-degree murder."

The anchor then gave a detailed account of the supposed burial of Julia Wills and sketched the probable manner in which two bags of fertilizer had been substituted for her body. She described how the belief of Wills's parents that Herbert Wills had poisoned their daughter became the catalyst that caused the alleged perpetrator, Baxter Cawthon, to attempt to dispose of the body at Proctor Creek. She described the murders of Donovan Grey and Garner Jakes in detail and added titillating bits about necrophiliac sex and sodomy.

She gave a pseudopsychological spin to Cawthon's penchant for impaling his victims, describing Grey hanging on the bamboo stake and Jakes lying pinned to the floor with a sword, and derived from those facts sexual implications involving the concept of penetration. She ended her story by pointing out that Ralph Hamlet, arrested the day before for having hidden his wife's body in his home, had exhibited behavior similar to Cawthon's in that both were unnaturally attracted to corpses. Her implied conclusion was that Hamlet was probably guilty of the same depraved sexual practices as Cawthon.

Fillmore, who had listened closely to the broadcast, shook his head with an exasperated expression. "I suppose that bitch is just doing her job. Unfortunately, it requires her to sensationalize the news for the sake of ratings. The fact that she was grossly unfair to you, Leda, and to Ralph Hamlet, didn't seem to faze her one bit. Well, broadcast journalists have never been noted for compassion, have they?"

Fulford was unwilling to condemn the reporter out of hand.

"She's got a point, I'm afraid. I was flustered, almost in a panic. I should have been able to talk some sense into Wills. But I couldn't. I failed."

"You're not Superwoman," Davis said. "What could you have done? People, especially cops, think they can always control events. That's nonsense. Sometimes things play out in their own way, no matter what."

"I suppose you're right, but I still have this nagging sense of failure."

Fillmore got up to leave. "That's because you're used to wearing a hair shirt." He paused, smiling at her. "You're due a lot of credit, Leda. You were the first one to realize Cawthon, not Hamlet, was the perpetrator. In my book, that's worth a lot of gold stars."

He stood at the door, twisting the knob back and forth, as if uncertain whether to go or stay. "Maybe this will make the two of you feel better—or worse. When the cops searched Cawthon's house and school, they found nothing to tie him to Julia Wills or to any other woman's body. Absolutely nothing to justify an indictment. Later, however, they discovered a safety deposit box at Bennet Bank containing a stash of jewelry presumably stolen from female victims whose bodies he got rid of somehow. I predict there will be a rash of exhumations when relatives identify that stuff. One item, Leda, was Julia Wills's wedding ring.

He stepped out the door and turned to close it.

"Oh. And one more positive note. Forensics is pretty sure, from preliminary results, that DNA samples will tie Cawthon to the rape of Wills and the sodomizing of Grey."

He still lingered, as if something more needed resolving.

Fulford smiled, savoring a small measure of satisfaction. She had impressed Fillmore, and that pleased her. She wondered if she had impressed Davis, too. His good opinion was more important to her than she cared to admit.

"What do you think will happen to Herbert Wills?" she asked before Fillmore closed the door.

"Not much. Even if he's indicted, something I doubt will happen, I think it would be impossible to convict him. He shot a man who had repeatedly violated his dead wife's body in a depraved way. What jury would vote to convict him for paying Cawthon back for that? Anyway, if indicted, he could plead self-defense, and you'd have to back him up on that, Leda."

"Yeah. With misgivings. If ever a man provoked an attack, Herbert Wills is that man. I think he planned it that way from the beginning. Provoke Cawthon, then shoot him."

"Probably. But what's your beef? Justice was done, wasn't it?" He closed the door.

Davis glanced at Fulford. "I was convinced Hamlet was our man. It bruised my ego a bit to be proven wrong. But I'll get over it, if you don't gloat."

"I wouldn't think of it," Fulford said gravely. "Gloating is bad manners."

"Would it be bad manners if you went with me to a late movie tonight?"

"Will you buy me a hamburger afterward?"

"With mustard, ketchup, onions, pickles, and anything else you can slather on it."

"Then I accept your offer. But I'll have to cancel my date with Chris," she said with a grin. "No problem. I can date him any time."

Wayne Minnick is the author of *The Art of Persuasion* and *Public Speaking* (Houghton Mifflin). He holds a Ph.D. in Speech Communication from Northwestern University, is a professor emeritus at Florida State University, and was an associate professor at Northwestern University. He began writing short stories and mystery novels upon retirement.